FEB 06 2012

BLACK ROCK CAÑON

**Center Point
Large Print**

Also by Les Savage, Jr. and available from Center Point Large Print:

West of Laramie
Doniphan's Thousand

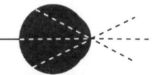

BLACK ROCK CAÑON

A Western Story

LES SAVAGE, JR.

CENTER POINT LARGE PRINT
THORNDIKE, MAINE

This Center Point Large Print edition is published
in the year 2012 in conjunction with
Golden West Literary Agency.

The text of this Large Print edition is unabridged.
In other aspects, this book may
vary from the original edition.
Printed in the United States of America.
Set in 16-point Times New Roman type.

ISBN: 978-1-61173-298-6

Library of Congress Cataloging-in-Publication Data

Savage, Les.
Black Rock Canon : a western story / Les Savage, Jr.
p. cm.
ISBN 978-1-61173-298-6 (library binding : alk. paper)
1. Large type books. I. Title.
PS3569.A826B55 2012
813′.54—dc23
                                          2011037083

Editor's Note

Les Savage, Jr., finished the short novel he titled "Gunmistress" at the end of June, 1948. He sent it to his agent, August Lenniger, who sent it on to Malcolm Reiss, the editor at Fiction House who loved Savage's stories and had been promoting him in Fiction House magazines since 1943. The top rate the magazine paid was 2¢ a word. Lenniger received a check for $800 on July 13, 1948. The short novel was published under the title "Lure of the Boothill Siren" in *Lariat Story Magazine* (5/49).

Fawcett Publications, which had had a line of pulp magazines and then comic books, launched their original paperback Gold Medal series in 1949. Savage's first hard cover novel, *Treasure of the Brasada*, was published by Simon and Schuster in 1947. Savage thought this short novel about a wild stallion could easily be expanded into a book-length novel. He got an assignment back of the short novel from Fiction House, and then completed work on the expansion, which he titled *Wild Horse Empire*. It ran a little over 52,000 words. Bill Lengel at Fawcett Gold Medal agreed to contract for the novel, offering a $1,000 advance, provided Savage make some significant changes in the story. "Lure of the Boothill Siren" was anything but a ranch romance, and neither was *Wild Horse Empire*. Bill Lengel wanted the story to be a ranch romance with the hero and heroine united at the end.

Savage acquiesced and rewrote the novel to give the editor what he wanted—even though it completely undermined the whole point of the story: how Aldis Spain and Blue Boy, the untamed roan, were very much alike. Even with having made the book into a ranch romance, Fawcett Gold Medal in their catalogue description kept something of Savage's original premise: "The horse or the girl! Which was more untamed—and more desirable?" *The Wild Horse* was issued as Gold Medal Book 111.

Universal-International bought screen rights to *The Wild Horse* and Geoffrey Holmes wrote the screenplay for what would be the third picture on Joel McCrea's three-picture contract with the studio. Of the three films, what was titled *Black Horse Canyon* (Universal-International, 1954) upon release, was McCrea's favorite, primarily because it cast him as a cowboy, a rôle he preferred over all others. Unfortunately in the press kit accompanying the film, the author of the original story was given as Lee Savage, Jr., and to this day that is how it usually appears in the film's credits.

Most writers have their models and for Savage his model for Aldis Spain was Ella Raines as she appeared in *Tall in the Saddle* (RKO, 1944), something evident in the descriptions of her in the book. In casting *Black Horse Canyon* the rôle of Aldis Spain was given to Universal contract player Mari Blanchard.

Fawcett Gold Medal wanted to do a new edition of *The Wild Horse* to be released in conjunction with the opening of the film as had previously been done so successfully with Louis L'Amour's novelization of James Edward Grant's screenplay for *Hondo* (Warner, 1953), which in turn had been based on a L'Amour short story. The book was retitled *Black Horse Canyon* when it was reprinted in 1954. Joel McCrea supplied the publisher with a blurb: "*Black Horse Canyon* is a novel that has captured the spirit and daring of the real West. It is my favorite Western and I got a real thrill out of playing the part of Rock in the Universal-International picture made from a book that I will never forget." It appeared as Gold Medal Book 411.

What appears here is Savage's book-length story as he originally wrote it—a far more compelling story than the ranch romance it was to become. However, rather than use Savage's original title, *Wild Horse Empire*, the title has been changed to Savage's first suggested alternative, *Black Rock Cañon*. It is on a ridge overlooking this cañon through which a creek flows that there is an old line shack where some of the most dramatic events between the characters occur.

Chapter One

Del Rockwall, together with Tie Taylor, had been up in Hellgate Strip for two weeks when he saw the blue horse. He was on a rocky ridge 1,000 feet above the valley floor, with the wildest, most unexplored section of Montana spilling off beneath his feet. It had rained during the morning, soaking Rockwall before he could get to his slicker. He was steaming now, as he dried out on the sun-heated rocks, with the rain clouds shredding northward about the towering peaks of the Garnets. These mountains flung their sullen, snow-peaked phalanxes away from Rockwall for fifty miles in an inexorable march to their meeting with the Sapphires in the north, at the apex of the gigantic triangle that was Hellgate Strip.

Rockwall had been scouting this section for the past few days, spotting the bands of wild horses, marking their water holes, their favorite directions of flight when they were flushed. As he studied the lower parks through his four-power cavalry binoculars, the seams deepened about his squinting eyes, seams holding years of weathering and the knowledge coming with a hard life that had started too young. Those raw, wandering years lay in the meager poorness of his gear—ancient Levi's, so worn across the seat and knees that they looked chalky white, a patched blue denim shirt that was still plastered damply against his back.

Interest kindled bright little lights in his smoky eyes as motion fluttered across the parks halfway down to the valley. Horses were moving in the timber down there. Back among the lodgepole pine and stunted tamarack they drifted like ghosts, heading toward the cañon, avoiding the open. Rockwall made an automatic estimate of time and distance. Once into the cañon, they'd pick up speed and move on downhill fast.

He returned to his horse, tightening the latigo and stepping on. Their trap was farther down, ten miles or so, and not yet completely ready. Going back to it, he'd still have a chance to watch this wild bunch when they hit the open, and find out how they maneuvered.

A mile distant, up on the slope, he paused to use the glasses again. He saw bays and browns, duns and pintos, mares with their colts, and a couple of young stallions. Then he saw the leader. A big, sleek-coated roan. Blue as a Colt barrel, sixteen hands high at least, each movement causing the muscles to leap and bunch and ripple across its heavy chest and flanks like the excited movement of live snakes.

Rockwall squinted intensely, the breath choked off in him by the unbelievable beauty of the beast. He had run wild ones off and on for most of his life, and he'd never seen a stallion to compare with this one. It was more than just the physical beauty. The vivid, untamed spirit of the animal seemed to reach out across the distance and clutch at him.

The shrill bugle of its call, warped by the wind, was carried to Rockwall, and the other horses turned obediently, seeking every shred of cover on the downhill trek to the cañon formed by two parallel spur ridges. Rockwall had not realized till now how hard his heart was hammering. A woman or two had brought this kind of excitement to him in the past. But never a horse.

The parallel struck him. A man could want this kind of horse as intensely as he could want a woman. He could feel the desire already forming in him. No horse runner who really meant to have an animal would take a chance of simply riding down and roping the one he wanted out of a wild herd. It was a 1,000 to one against success. And if he missed, he might spook the horses so far away that he'd be lucky even to catch sight of them for six months to come.

Yet one look at the blue roan seemed to have robbed Rockwall of ordinary calculation. He only knew that he had to see the animal again, as a man would follow a beautiful woman through a crowd for another glimpse of her. And if he found himself in a position to take a stab at it, he meant to try for the roan. That was all the more reason to finish work on the trap.

Rockwall was a short, compact man in his thirties. He was just finishing work on the trap, when young Tie Taylor brought his steel dust mare down through the plumed Montana bear grass and halted it close by, dropping the words casually in his soft Texas drawl. "Three horse-backers been watching us a long time from up on that westerly ridge."

Del Rockwall stopped lashing the top bar in place against the gatepost of the pen and looked up at Tie.

"Maybe we better meet them fully dressed," he said, moving over to where he had hung his gun belt on the bar of the pen he had just completed.

"I don't see why you always go for your dewey," grumbled Tie good-naturedly. "I never seen anybody with a neck so full of hell. Folks ain't got as much vinegar in them as you make out."

"They even got less when you're wearing hardware." Rockwall smiled thinly, watching the boy dismount.

Tie leaned casually against the pen, shoving his great Stetson back to reveal a mane of hair yellow as corn. His eyes were blue and guileless in a smooth, handsome face, and there was a casual, youthful recklessness to the slouch of his long body, with its hips so narrow and its shoulders so wide. The bull-hide chaps slung on his saddle horn made no concession to the Cheyenne cut of this northern country; they were old batwings laced with brush scars, as Texan as the double-rigged kak on his mare.

Rockwall had buckled on his gun belt and was turning back to finish lashing on the last bar, when the white plumes of the bear grass began to sway again. Tie raised his head a little, staring at something Rockwall could not see yet, and the strange expression on his face chilled Rockwall.

The woman came through the tall grass on the most beautiful Appaloosa Rockwall had ever seen. The broad chest and sleek barrel were a dark, dappled blue, fading gradually into a creamy blanket over the rump. Red spots covered this in an even pattern, as if some painter had daubed them there. The woman herself was stunning. The long jet bob of black hair formed a rippling, curling frame for her face.

Her black eyes were large, arresting, and there was something infinitely sensuous to her ripe underlip. The throaty chuckle stirred an alabaster throat faintly, filled with a calculating seduction.

"Gentlemen," she said in an amused, mocking way.

"I guess I'm in heaven," gasped Tie in deceptive naïveté. "I ain't never seen such a beautiful woman before, and I ain't never been called a gentleman."

"I'm Aldis Spain from the Forked Tongue," she murmured.

"Tie Taylor from Fort Worth," said the boy.

"Is there any other city?" she asked.

"No, ma'am," Tie told her soberly.

Rockwall had stood silently through it all, none of Tie's gaping admiration in his appraisal of the woman. She turned to him. Her smile held the same indulgent condescension it had for the boy, but there was a vague, irritated disturbance behind it. He saw now that she was younger than she first appeared.

"The silent one," she told Rockwall. "I never trusted the type."

"Del likes to figure things out," Tie told her.

"I was wondering where your friends were," Rockwall said.

"Kenny Graves," she told him, "will be along. Maybe you can figure him out."

Even as she spoke, the two riders were pushing their animals from the bear grass behind her. The leader forked a nervous, stockinged black. The man was not over average height, but there was something vividly commanding about his figure. His boots looked bench-made and his foxed pants and steel pen coat were impeccably tailored. The weathering of open range would never leave his face, although the coloring had faded before a more recent life of greater ease. His black eyes had the direct stab of a knife, and his

14

words left his hard, thin lips in a staccato blast.

"Why did you do that, Aldis?"

"Maybe I wanted to see them first," the woman pouted. "The boy is cute."

The look the man cast at Tie was involuntary reaction to her words. Then, almost in anger, he switched his glance to Rockwall. He seemed to settle himself deliberately, pulling a slim cigar from the breast pocket of his blue coat, biting off the end as he bit off his words. Spitting it out, he spoke to Rockwall.

"Rockwall and Taylor, *hmm?* We heard you were looking to run some wild horses up this way. You should have seen me before going to all this trouble. You've built your trap in the wrong pasture."

"You Kenneth Graves?" asked Rockwall.

The man nodded, poked his unlit cheroot at the other rider. "And this is Tony Laroque. He does things for me."

Rockwall's eyes passed across Laroque in a swift, casual way. The man's clothes were rougher than Graves's—brass-studded Levi's whitened with dust, a denim ducking jacket with a small, blackened hole in one sleeve. His greasy hair was tied in a queue with a strip of rawhide, and his eyes met Rockwall's with insolent, heavy-lidded reserve.

"We had it on government authority this was open range," Rockwall said.

15

Graves smiled thinly. "The Land Office isn't infallible. This strip belongs to the Forked Tongue."

"I don't see how it could," interposed Tie. "I saw the government survey maps. The Forked Tongue couldn't dab onto Hellgate Strip. The only way it could be owned is through homesteading, and it hasn't been opened yet."

Graves condescended to indicate Tie with his cigar. "You got a smart boy here."

"He gets around," said Rockwall. "Why don't you try a different horse? You handle stock yourself maybe, and you got sort of a monopoly on the horse running around Hellgate."

"You're even smarter," said Graves, smiling with his mouth.

"What gives you the monopoly?" asked Rockwall.

"I have a government contract."

"The only contracts they give is to buy the animals at a shipping point," Rockwall told him. "They don't care who catches them."

Graves took his cigar out, studying it. "You have too many marbles for this business, Rockwall. Most horse runners are such dumb bunnies."

"And you've been able to push them off without too much trouble," said Rockwall.

"I usually don't have too much trouble even with the smart ones," Graves told him. "How about a deal? I have quite a few men running horses around here. But none with your reputation. I'll give you five dollars a head and a place to bunk."

"When we can get ten dollars a head ourselves?" asked Rockwall. "I don't think you have many horse runners in your string, Graves. I don't think you're as big an operator as you talk. You wouldn't bother making any deal if you were. There's enough country around Hellgate for an army of horse runners. What's so valuable about this strip? The blue roan?"

Graves could not help sucking in his breath and leaning forward against his saddle horn. The woman's chuckle came, throaty and amused.

"You do have a biscuit cutter here, Kenny," she told Graves. Then she was looking at Rockwall. "How did you know about Blue Boy? There aren't half a dozen men in the world who've seen him."

"He's blue as a Colt barrel and he's powerful big," Rockwall told her. "I spotted him earlier today down Black Rock Cañon. What makes him so valuable? Maybe Jennings over at the Forked Tongue has a standing offer for him. Would a thousand dollars be too much for a horse like that?"

Graves was leaning even farther toward Rockwall, staring at him in disbelief. "How the hell did you know about Jennings? You haven't been around here before?"

"I spent an evening in your Hellgate saloons,"

Rockwall told him. "A man can learn a lot if he keeps his ears clean and his eyes open."

"He's liable to get them full of sand if he keeps them open too wide," said Graves. "I'll ask you to get out of Hellgate Strip, now, Rockwall. The next time I come back I won't be asking."

"We spent a lot of time on this trap," said Rockwall. "I don't think we'll go till we get a band or two."

Tony Laroque shifted in the saddle, and Aldis Spain drew in a sharp, excited breath. But Rockwall had already turned toward the man.

"You got anything on your mind?"

"Tony isn't paid to think," said Graves. "In fact, he even leaves his feelings up to me. If I told him to like you, he would."

"And you'd only tell him to like us if we got out."

"You could always say you had a good friend back in Hellgate."

"We're not getting out."

Graves turned to Laroque, pointing his cigar at Rockwall. "I want you to dislike this man."

"That won't be hard," answered Laroque.

"Come on, Aldis," said Graves, swinging his horse around.

"I'm sorry I won't be here the next time Kenny comes," Aldis told Rockwall, before wheeling her mount. Then she smiled at Tie. "It's too bad. You were so good-looking, too."

The moon was a painter, splashing the earth with a pot full of yellow ochre. The wolves were singers, filling the night with their mournful chorus. The brush was an audience, applauding in ghostly whispers with each passage of wind.

Rockwall and Tie rode through it three hours after Graves had left them. The pen was finished and they were on their way to the pools up in the Garnets where the wild horses would drink near dawn. Rockwall had worked it all out, even to the ridge leading into the trap. Nine out of ten wild ones would run the length of a ridge if they ever attained it, and the men had planted their spooks to drive this bunch right up onto the high, narrow hogback. It was Tie who spoke finally, as they left the badlands of Hellgate Strip and began rising into the mountains.

"That gal was prettier'n a tabby cat on a pink pillow."

"You always put your mind on the wrong side of things," Rockwall told him.

Tie chuckled. "You was too busy reading her past history to see her face. I'll bite, what was it?"

"A lot of men, and a lot of trouble," said Rockwall. He turned in the saddle. "Maybe we *had* better pull out."

"Now, Del," protested Tie. "You know I'll sit out any pot Graves wants to play for. As for the gal, don't worry about me. You want to get that blue roan pretty bad, don't you? Blue Boy. Now you know his name. Where did you find out about him before you saw him?"

"You heard the same things I did in those Hellgate saloons."

"I didn't hear no mention of Blue Boy."

"You heard the girl say how few men actually knew of his existence," said Rockwall. "But they talked all around him. That bartender, for instance, telling what a horse fancier this Black Jack Jennings is, over on the Forked Tongue."

"I don't see what that has to do with it," said Tie. "I can't put things together the way you do, Rock."

"Any man who likes horseflesh as much as Jennings would pay a good price for an animal like that blue roan if he knew about it. Graves was so interested in shooing us out of Hellgate Strip today, I figured somebody must have been making it worth his while. Graves worked for Jennings before he took to running horses himself. Add up?"

Tie began to laugh, a soft, chuckling sound that pushed his belly spasmodically against his belt. "I never saw a man for figuring out the story like you." He sobered. "Would this Blue Boy fetch a big enough price to pay down on that horse ranch you're always dreaming about?"

"Just about."

"Then what say we show Kenny Graves what horse running really looks like."

Rockwall dropped Tie at a station they had already chosen for him, about halfway up to the watering places. Then Rockwall climbed on into the Garnets until reaching a pool that had shown signs of regular use by the horses. He got off his horse in some alders upwind from the water, easing the cinch some, and settled down for the wait. They would come near dawn, and it wasn't much past midnight now. He found thoughts of Aldis Spain drifting into his mind somehow, with the picture of those passionate lips. Despite a deep distrust she had stirred in him, he could not help the poignant attraction her beauty held. There had been too many women like that in his past. They almost formed landmarks along the trail he and Tie had followed up from Texas. How many tights had he pulled the reckless kid out of? He must have dozed then. He came awake with a fresh, cool breeze in his face, and the moonlight gone.

His horse's head was lifted, and he stood to pull the noseband tight, preventing the whinny that pulsed up in its throttle. They were already drifting in down there, shadowy beasts in an eerie world of false dawn, wary, high-stepping wild ones, thrusting their heads constantly this way and that to peer and sniff, taking quick, furtive nips at the water. The sight always gave him a great exhilaration. There was something so primeval about it, so untouched by man.

He tugged his latigo up to tighten the cinch and

stepped aboard his pony, moving slowly into the open. A dozen heads raised. A neigh floated against him on the breeze. They turned like a well-trained platoon and started drifting.

He did not push them hard. The running would come later. As long as he moved slowly and kept a distance, he could move them along in the direction he had chosen. He looked in vain for the blue roan. He shrugged. That would be too much to ask. True dawn showed the leader to be a line-back buckskin in his prime. That was good. And two or three good-looking mares.

On down off the Garnets and into the badlands of the Strip, he pursued them. Gnarled gullies and rocky hogbacks barren of timber. A tight little valley filled with the gurgle of the stream running on down into Clark Fork. Then the ridge was in sight.

"Hay-ah!" shouted Rockwall, and put a boot heel against his horse. It had been a wild one once, too. He had picked it up mustanging down on the *llanos*, and hadn't found another one since with as much guts or bottom. It went into its gallop, and the whole bunch was running.

They headed down the top of that ridge like a train going down a track. He knew Tie would pick them up now and, without wasting his horse in the climb to the top of the ridge, turned to run as hard as he could across the flats parallel to their line of flight. It allowed him to reach the pen ahead of them. The trap was on the opposite slope of the ridge, and, if he bulged over the top from this side, it would turn them right into the wings.

His pony scrambled up through shale and talus under the touch of spurs. He came on top of the ridge about twenty yards ahead of them. The stallion saw him and veered sharply down the offside. With Tie yelling like an Indian behind them, they ran right in between the wing fences of the trap. Rockwell ran in on this flank, and then both men went mad to give them the final push through the gate, yelling and screaming and slapping their hats against their legs. This hullabaloo must have drowned out the gunshots.

Rockwall didn't hear anything. He only felt the jolt of his pony beneath him. It was an unmistakable sensation, and he started kicking free of the oxbows even before the animal stumbled and went head over heels. He lit rolling, smashing through buckbrush and over a boulder that sent a great nauseous wave of pain through him.

He finally came to a stop, choking in the dust, each spasmodic inhalation causing him to grimace. He lay there without trying to get up, until he had his old Hopkins and Allen out. His pony lay dead twenty yards away, with blood from the gunshot making a dark stain against the pale of its buckskin chest. That brought his first anger. It had been a good horse.

The wild ones were milling crazily in the gate of the trap, and turning back this way. He had to get from between the wings quickly or be run down in their flight back out. He rose and started stumbling downslope. His breath had a groaning sound, coming in. He had only taken two or three steps when the shots broke out again.

Dust kicked up, white and deadly, a foot from him. The horses were coming back, whinnying and squealing shrilly. He had his choice of being run down by them or heading on into the shots. He started zigzagging in his run downslope, and, when the gun smashed again, the bullet kicked up dust farther away from him than the first shot had. Then the whole bunch of wild mustangs was on him and he had to dive and roll again, crying out involuntarily as a hoof on the fringe of the band caught his shoulder a glancing blow.

He rolled into red monkey grass, free of the stampeding horses, and stopped flopping over at the bottom of the slope. There was a gully here, snarled with willows and alders. Before Rockwall could gain his feet once more, a voice reached him.

"Did the horses get him?"

"Looked like it," answered another in a voice like the hoarse boom of a bullfrog. "Now let's get Texas. We've got him boxed in."

"You ain't getting anybody," Rockwall found himself growling, as he pawed to his feet and crashed into the alders. He saw them as furtive, shadowy movements through the trees, converging on some spot ahead. He picked the one on his left and began shooting. He was close enough now to distinguish them in the timber. Both men turned toward him with swift, surprised motions, losing their impetus forward, and his second shot brought a hoarse shout from the one on his left, and the movement there disappeared abruptly with a crashing sound of brush.

"Del?" It was Tie's voice.

"Hold on, boy, I'm coming."

"Don't stick your neck out, Del."

That meant Tie was in real trouble. The worse off he was, the less favors he would ask. The rest was finished in the crackling sound of brush smashed in the passage of running and the deafening thunder of guns and the wild, hoarse shout of that remaining man as he realized Rockwall had come up behind. He snapped a shot at Rockwall. Rockwall ran on, emptying his gun at the shadowy figure. At the same time, Tie's gun began smashing from behind the man. He must have broken and run because he was no longer ahead of Rockwall, in the smoke and the noise.

"All right, Tie, it's me!" called Rockwall. Tie stopped shooting and Rockwall found him lying in a mat of buckbrush. There was a grin on his face and a pool of blood beneath him.

"They nicked me," he said. "Who was it?"

Rockwall was dabbing at the blood with his neckerchief to get some idea of the wound. "I don't know. I think I tagged one, but they're gone now."

"Do I put my saddle in a sack?" asked Tie.

"It'll take more than this to kill you," said Rockwall. Then his voice took on a deadly flat tone. "If anybody sacks his saddle, it'll be Kenny Graves."

Chapter Two

Their camp was located in a birch and aspen grove above the creek, about a mile north of the trap. It consisted of a brush lean-to with a tarp stretched over it to keep out the last of the spring rains. They reached it in the gray dawn, with Tie riding his mare and Rockwall walking and carrying his own saddle.

Tie had lost a lot of blood and could barely sit the saddle. Rockwall had examined the wound back at the trap and knew the boy needed a doctor. The bullet had buried itself in his shoulder, and Rockwall had been unable to get it out. As soon as he reached camp, he got one of his spare animals that he had left staked in the coulée, throwing on the saddle. Then he padded a blanket over Tie's saddle horn so the boy could lie across it without being hurt, and fashioned hobbles beneath the mare's barrel to hold Tie's feet.

"We're going to the Forked Tongue," Rockwall said. "You need a bed and a sawbones."

The boy grinned feebly. "I'd ride clear across Montana for another look at that gal."

Rockwall put a lead rope on the mare and mounted up, heading north. They had ridden an hour before the sun topped the eastern peaks, quickly burning the night's chill away. An hour after this they reached the spot where Black Rock Cañon forked, the right branch heading toward the town of Hellgate, the left branch carrying the brawling mountain creek up into the Garnets.

Black Jack Jennings had been one of the first to bring Texas cattle to Montana. He had weathered many reverses to emerge one of the biggest operators in the state. His holdings ran eastward from the town of Hellgate for uncounted miles, bounded on the north by the Blackfoot River, on the south by Clark Fork, with the towering Garnets forming a backbone of summer ranges for his cattle.

They dropped out of the first range of mountains into a broad sage flat and met a three-strand fence marching from horizon to horizon. They rode this to a poor man's gate, passed through, and pushed on. Tie was lying forward on the horse now, half conscious, his face caked with alkali. Cattle bearing Jennings's brand on their flanks began to appear in small bunches. Then they passed into the mountains again. It was afternoon when they finally came within sight of the ranch. There was a big house set high on a knoll, as rough and bleak and domineering as the man himself. It occupied the highest eminence in miles, facing north, a gesture as unmistakably defiant as a brandished fist.

The other buildings were grouped about it lower down, corrals, barns, bunkhouse, and cook shack, built of unpeeled logs that blended roughly into the rugged landscape. Dust raised by a man working a horse in one of the corrals lay in a tawny patina over the pattern of pens and outbuildings.

As Rockwall passed the pole fence with Tie, he saw that it was a white-headed rider within the corral. The man was trotting a chestnut around the pen, fighting it every foot of the way. The other hands, gathered down one length of the fence, turned a row of weather-roughened faces, each one holding a carefully withdrawn speculation that bordered on hostility.

Rockwall halted in the hard-packed yard before the long stone porch, with the heat pressing against him like a smothering blanket. Black Jack Jennings sat in a hide-bottomed chair on the porch, making no move to rise or greet them. On a low table beside him were a moisture-beaded pitcher and a glass. In his left hand he gripped a fly swatter. He took an absent swipe at a buzzing fly with this, squinting down at Tie Taylor, who lolled forward across the mare, arms dangling.

"What's wrong with the boy?"

"A bullet. He needs a doctor, Mister Jennings."

"There's one down at Hellgate."

A muscle twitched in Rockwall's face. "He's in no shape to be taken that far. Any more punishment like this and he could easily die. It won't cost you anything to send a hand to Hellgate after the sawbones."

"I'm running a ranch, not a hospital."

"He's out of Texas," snapped Rockwall. "So are you. Doesn't that count for anything?"

A murky expression moved through Jennings's stony features. He turned his face partly away, as if to hide it, staring at the pitcher as he picked it up and filled the glass. Rockwall hoped he had found one of the man's weak points. No matter how long they had been gone, most Texans took a fierce pride in their heritage, a pride that might lie buried in even a man like Jennings. He took a deep drink.

"No," he said, with a shake of his massive head. "I didn't pile up what I got by playing good Samaritan to wild young hellions out of Texas. Every other man who's come north of Red River was prodded from behind. It'd take all the rope in the state to hang them if they went home again."

29

Rockwall shifted carefully in the saddle. "You're too damned loose with that kind of talk. I didn't leave Texas with a rope waiting for me. Why did you leave?"

He had meant to goad Jennings. The big man's eyes fluttered in wrinkled anger. For a moment he was still, with his acerbic breathing splaying out his whitened nostrils. Then the fly swatter began to wave again, and Rockwall discovered for the first time what its movement had kept him from seeing earlier. There was a holstered gun on the table behind the pitcher.

"Stranger," said Jennings at last, "there's a graveyard about a mile south of here. You get a civil tongue in your head fast, or your face is going to be patted with a shovel."

The man had spoken in a loud, hoarse tone that carried to the corrals, and now Rockwall heard the beginnings of movement down there.

"I wouldn't count too much on your crew," he told Jennings. "If your ramrod is any example, the whole bunch of them aren't worth an old McCarty."

Jennings leaned forward sharply, staring at Rockwall. "What's wrong with my ramrod?"

"He's ruining that chestnut so she'll never answer the bit," Rockwall told him.

"I don't believe it." Jennings leaned back in his chair. "Baxter's topped some of the toughest bronc's in Montana."

"Any fool with a little nerve can top the rough string," snapped Rockwall. "It looked to me like that chestnut was in the gentling stage. From what I've seen, Baxter hasn't got any right being within half a mile of a horse at that point."

Jennings half closed his lids, staring beyond Rockwall for a moment. This abrupt change in the man would have been surprising to anybody who did not know a horse lover. Rockwall had already seen enough of Jennings's brutality to suspect that the man's love of horses had to be a warped one, motivated more by a desire for possession than by a true feeling for the animals. Yet, twisted as it was, it might still dominate him as passionately as it would a man who really loved the animals, submerging everything else, as it had submerged his anger now.

"Baxter *has* been having trouble with that chestnut," Jennings muttered. "And a couple of other beauties I wanted polished off." His eyes focused suddenly on Rockwall. "I've heard of you. Name's RockwAll, isn't it? John Mingo was up last spring from Fort Worth."

Rockwall nodded. "I worked for Mingo a year or so."

"He said you had no right simply running the wild ones," Jennings told him. "Said your talent lay in gentling them. Trouble is, you were too damned independent to work for somebody else very long, and you couldn't ever get a big enough stake on your own to set up in business. He told me you were a wizard when it came to polishing off the broke ones."

Rockwall studied the man's heavy, square face. "What's on your mind?"

"A deal," said Jennings. "I'll give your pard a bed under my roof, if you'll do a job for me. I've got a whole string like that chestnut I'd like polished off."

"You wouldn't just take the boy in out of your goodness of heart?" asked Rockwall sardonically.

Jennings's face flushed. "I'm making a business deal. You taking it or not?"

Rockwall looked at Tie's slack body and shrugged. "I guess I'll have to. This boy's got to get in a bed."

At this moment the door of the big house came open, and Aldis Spain stepped out. She was obviously just out of bed, her blinking, heavily lidded eyes lending her face the slumberous provocation of a sleepy child. She was fumbling to belt a yellow robe over her nightdress, its lace hem whispering about bare feet, but at sight of Tie she forgot this and hurried down the steps. In the merciless light of the hot sun, no flaw appeared in the satiny texture of her face, but her heavy dark brows were curled into an angry frown.

"Your talking woke me up. What are you wasting time like this for?" Her hand rested gently on Taylor's forehead, a maternal concern making her eyes luminous. "He's burning up with fever," she said, whirling hotly on Jennings. "Uncle, we have to get him off this horse and into the house."

Anger turned Jennings's face a mottled red. Rockwall saw his hands move and close into fists. Then a helpless expression drained the anger from his face.

Rockwall looked from the big man to his niece, realizing what might lie between them. Jennings had apparently brought everything else in his world to heel with the pressure of his brutal strength. But the spirit of Aldis Spain was perhaps something he could not conquer with his bare hands, as much as he might want to.

"You get him in, Rockwall," Jennings said thickly. "I'll go down and tell Baxter to ride for the doctor."

Rockwall unhobbled Tie and slid him off the mare. He was still conscious, although delirious, and, between them, Rockwall and Aldis managed to get him in the house on his feet. It was dark inside, and cool. The living room ran across the front of the house, wainscoted as high as a man's head with undressed pine logs.

They went down a long hall and into a bedroom at its far end. Rockwall grunted with surprise, recognizing this as the girl's own room. It looked as a hotel room might, when someone meant to use it for a night or two and then move on. It hadn't been lived in. There were bags beside a chest of drawers and a few things hung in a closet, but no pictures on the walls and none of the personal effects the girl might have been expected to scatter about to make the place more livable.

Aldis smoothed the covers of her bed, and Rockwall lowered Taylor. Aldis tugged at his boots. Rockwall stepped back, and noticed Jennings had followed him and was leaning against the door frame.

"Baxter's on his way," the big man growled. "Aldis can do what's necessary here till the sawbones shows up. Meanwhile, that chestnut is still saddled down at the corral."

Rockwall felt the weariness of a sleepless night and the grueling ride drag at his shoulders. He took a heavy breath, cinching up his belt.

"You drive a hard bargain, Jennings. Maybe one will snap back in your face someday."

The man's grin held no humor. "I haven't met a man who could snap it yet."

Aldis turned from the bed to cast a heavy-lidded glance at Rockwall. "Don't speak too soon, Uncle Black Jack," she murmured.

Chapter Three

With a night's sleep and a big breakfast making him feel like a new man, Rockwall stepped out of the cook shack into the hot sunlight of another morning. He had eaten before Jennings's riders were up, and now they were streaming from the bunkhouse in a growling, blinking line, drawn by the smell of hot coffee and wood smoke that filled the morning air. Rockwall avoided them, heading up to the main house to see how Tie was. He crossed the compound and reached the porch to find Black Jack Jennings having breakfast there.

Jennings was like an old Texas mossyhorn, rolling in tallow with age and rich graze, but still showing the restless, vital virility of his younger years in the great, broad-shouldered frame. He had a mane of white hair and brows like hoarfrost above eyes filled this morning with twinkling blue humor. His sounds were like a bull, rich and rambling.

"Boy's still asleep, if that's what you came up for," he said. "Spent a restless night, but I think he's all right now." He grunted as he leaned forward to open a cigar box on the table before his chair. "You smoke these?"

Rockwall took one of the cigars from the box, clipping it with care and lighting up with a match from the table.

"A man with appreciation for good tobacco and good horses is damned scarce in this country, Rockwall," Jennings said around a mouthful of bacon and eggs. "I liked the way you quieted down that chestnut yesterday. You were right about Baxter. He had the beast almost ruined."

Rockwall was hardly listening. He had absently taken a chunk of battered lead from his pocket and was hefting it in his hand.

"That the bullet the sawbones dug out of Tie?" grunted Jennings.

"Forty-Four," murmured Rockwall.

The cattleman snorted. "Nine out of ten riders pack that caliber. It won't lead you to the man who did it. You'd stand more chance of finding him by sticking around here and keeping your ears open." Jennings put his fork down. "How'd you like to ramrod the Forked Tongue for me?"

Rockwall had not been completely unprepared for this. "How about Baxter?" he said.

"Soft steel when I need a cutting edge," growled Jennings. "His job's yours if you want it."

Rockwall sent an oblique glance at him. "You're not trying to hire a foreman, Jennings. What is it you really want?"

"Accept my offer and I'll tell you."

"That means taking your orders, and I'm

through doing that, from any man," Rockwall said. "I'll work your horses for you till Tie's well enough to travel. Maybe I'd better go down and get started right now."

"Hold it," said Jennings, pushing himself out of the chair with a grunt and rising. He stood there a moment, close to Rockwall, breathing stertorously with a full stomach and the rich living of these last years. "The man who was foreman of this outfit before Baxter was Kenny Graves," he said at last. Jennings shrugged. "He was a good man at the time, but he started running stuff for himself. He quit me finally to go into business himself. Got so rich running the wild ones now he's bought himself a saloon."

"Met him."

"How so?"

"We had a run-in with him along the Hellgate Strip. He didn't want anybody else tagging Blue Boy."

"You know about the roan, too?"

"I saw him," said Rockwall. "What did you offer Graves for the horse?"

"Fifteen hundred?"

"Is he worth it?"

"And more," said Jennings. "Any cattleman in Montana would give it if they knew about him. He keeps to such a wild part of the Strip he's known to very few. Funny thing, Rockwall . . ."

—Jennings's eyes had taken on a distant,

luminous focus, as if looking at something beyond Rockwall's vision—"funny thing about him. Everybody who's seen him seems to get a bug. They can't forget him. I've got a right smart passion about him. I'd give almost anything to get my hands on him. Graves is the same way. We broke up over that animal. Oh"—he shrugged, mouthing it—"there was other trouble, as I've said. But it all started the first time he saw Blue Boy and wanted him for himself. It seems to get a man, somehow. There's even talk of an old horse runner out in the Garnets who's gone crazy over the animal and tries to kill anyone who gets near enough to nab Blue Boy. Graves claims to have been shot at by the man."

"With a voice like a frog?" said Rockwall.

Jennings grinned. "You thinking of the man who shot Tie?"

Rockwall shrugged. "I'll know him next time I hear him. With a voice like that. Graves have a friend to fill the bill?"

"Doesn't sound familiar." Jennings leaned forward and put an hand on Rockwall's shoulder. "You won't spread this, Rockwall. Every horse runner in a hundred miles would be in there trying to get Blue Boy, if he was known. He's got the most beautiful mixture of Morgan and Quarter you can imagine. A get from him would give you the best all-round string in the state. Even if you don't consider the get, he'd be worth it himself."

"I'll keep the war bag laced up." Rockwall smiled.

"Now Graves is working up another deal." Jennings dropped his hand. "He'll sell me Blue Boy, if he gets him. Only he don't want money for the animal. How much more have I got to say to put it into words for you?"

Rockwall frowned at Jennings. "Aldis?" he said.

"What else?" asked Jennings roughly. "Graves doesn't need money any more."

"Are you talking about trading Aldis for that horse?" A tense disbelief was in Rockwall's voice.

"*I* am not," Jennings insisted. "But it's what she wants . . . to get away from me. If she doesn't leave me for Graves, it'll be somebody else."

"So you hope somebody . . . anybody . . . gets Blue Boy before Aldis does leave you, so you can trade her for the blue roan?" Rockwall's voice was barely audible.

"Not Graves. He's poison. But how does that kind of proposition appeal to you, Rockwall?"

"What do you think?" Rockwall asked softly.

"Maybe money wouldn't influence you, either," Jennings said. "Maybe because I think you're more interested in Aldis than you let on."

"So you'd trade your niece to me if I was to get Blue Boy before Graves did?"

Jennings licked his lips, and Rockwall saw an avid light fill his eyes. "I want no part of Graves, and I don't want Aldis seeing him. But look at it this way. I've always got what I wanted out of life till that horse came along. Call it an obsession, call it anything you like. That blue roan is in my blood to the point where I'm going to have him at any price. And you're the man who can get him for me."

Rockwall carefully ground out the glowing tip of the cigar against the porch railing and placed the dead smoke on the table.

"I made a deal to smooth out some saddle stock for you, Jennings," he said. "That's enough for me."

"Rockwall . . ."

But Rockwall was already going down the steps, and he did not turn back. He crossed the barren compound, filled with disgust for a man who would use his niece as a pawn in such a game as that.

Chapter Four

The corrals and barns made a haphazard pattern in the lower meadows. Baxter was waiting for him in front of the bunkhouse. Rockwall noticed the telltale tracings of whiskey veins in the man's nose and the slack fold of fat rimming his belt. He made Rockwall think of an albino horse.

His hair was so blond it looked white, his smooth youthful face bore the perpetual ruddy glow of skin that would not tan, and his eyes were as blank and expressionless as china.

Baxter snorted. "You must have sold Jennings a bill of goods. You can't pet horses like they was kittens. You got to show them who's boss. Just because you were lucky with that chestnut yesterday doesn't mean it'll last."

"That your little speech for the morning?" asked Rockwall.

Baxter flushed, starting a step toward Rockwall. Then he settled back, jerked his head toward the barn, and turned to lead the way inside.

They came to a man forking hay into a wheelbarrow. He had on a white shirt, soiled with dirt and droppings, and his undershot jaw was covered with several days' stubble.

"Potter, get Garnet out and saddled," Baxter ordered.

Potter looked up, and in the semi-gloom his expression was one of surprise. He put aside his fork and moved toward a stall down the aisle. Rockwall followed, studying the animal in the stall. It was a mare, over sixteen hands, with a coat the color of blood. She began to shift around nervously, steel shod hoofs *clicking* like castanets.

"One of Jennings's pets," Baxter told him, a jeering note in his voice. "She's strictly for riding, but she hasn't been worked much lately. A lot of high spirits in her. Needs quieting down."

"Yeah," snickered Potter from behind them. "Yeah."

Rockwall hardly heard this. He was looking into the next stall. The horse there had shifted to reveal a white rump daubed with red spots. This was the Appaloosa that Aldis Spain had been riding in the hills. Now she had been riding it again recently. It stood hipshot and lathered, like an animal worked to the limit of its endurance.

Potter put the saddle on the mare in the stall, then led her out. The sun was still bringing early morning steam up out of the earth in the corral, bearing with it the decaying odors of old horse droppings and trampled dirt.

Potter held the bridle while Rockwall stepped on. The red beast began fidgeting and snorting. Rockwall put a boot in her flank. Garnet responded instantly, almost pitching him over the rolled cantle with her first arching leap. He pulled in and laid the reins against her neck. She reacted with a galvanic burst of motion, tucking her chin in without changing direction. In another instant she would crash into the corral fence. Using an old Mexican trick, Rockwall dug his spurs in hard and hauled back on the reins. Disorganized by these contradictory signals—the spurs to go ahead, the hauled-back reins to halt—she screamed and twisted to one side, rearing up as though trying to climb away from the pain of his rowels.

When the horse rose so high that he thought she would go on over backward, Rockwall released pressure on the reins and hit her in the neck with his fist. Once, twice, three times, literally knocking the animal back down again. He felt muscles bunch for bucking, but, before she could do this, he pulled the reins in again and swung off.

"You don't have to be so damned rough with her!" called Baxter, running toward Rockwall. "Jennings finds blood on her he'll have a fit."

Rockwall ignored him, going to the head of the quivering, shying beast. He got her mouth open with difficulty.

"Who's been working this animal?" he asked.

"I have," said Baxter. "Why?"

"You've been laying on that bit so much she's got an iron mouth already. I'm going to take this bit out and try a hackamore."

"Don't be a fool, you'll never be able to hold her," Baxter said hoarsely.

"Use iron in her mouth much longer and you won't even hold her with a bit," said Rockwall. "I'll take the responsibility, Baxter."

The man stared at him, a flush turning that albino flesh even more ruddy. "It's a lot of responsibility, Rockwall."

"You aimed to see me mashed against a fence," Rockwall said. "I'm not here to make an issue of things, Baxter. I like to get along with everybody. If it works, and anybody was to ask me, I'll tell them the hackamore was your suggestion. If it doesn't work, it was mine. Now I'll ride her my way."

The tension left Baxter's shoulders slowly. Finally he turned and walked toward the barn. Rockwall told Potter to hold Garnet, and followed the man. He was far enough behind so that, when Baxter ducked into the barn, there were still a few steps for Rockwall to take. He had not reached the door before he heard the voice.

"You've got Garnet out, Ward. You're not trying to work her?"

"New hand's working her, Miss Spain."

"Ward, don't be a fool. Garnet will kill him."

"Will he, Miss Spain?" asked Rockwall from the doorway.

She wheeled in the musty, inner gloom of the small room, and her eyes were immense black pools of surprise. For a moment, he allowed himself to realize that she looked even more beautiful than the last time. That midnight hair was in an upsweep coiffure with a jade comb holding it high. She had on a short-sleeved shirt, with the top button unfastened to create a deep V that focused attention on the taut way the starched white cloth was drawn across the swell of her breasts. Her khaki riding britches were not jodhpurs. They fitted her leg like another layer of skin, outlining the curve of a mature hip.

"What were you getting, Ward?" she asked finally.

"A hackamore for Garnet." Baxter hesitated a moment, then went on hastily. "It wasn't my idea, Miss Spain, I give you my word, this man . . ."

"I imagine, Ward, I imagine." She emitted that sensuous, throaty chuckle. "It was Mister Rockwall's idea. All right. Why don't you get it? I'd like to see what Mister Rockwall can do to that devil with a hackamore. I'd really like to see."

Baxter glanced at Rockwall, moved over to the rope harnesses hanging on their wooden racks. He reached for one of three-eighths hemp, but Rockwall grunted in a negative way.

"Give me that pepper-and-salt one with the big knot."

"Regular Mexican, ain't you?" muttered Baxter. He got it off the hook and turned, without offering to move farther. Aldis regarded him in a waiting, smiling way, and finally he got the idea. He left the barn reluctantly.

Then the woman was looking at Rockwall with that smile. She moved toward him until her breasts almost touched his chest, looking up into his eyes. She reached up with one hand to run a pale, soft finger down under his collar in a confiding way.

"Look," she murmured on a husky breath, "I can help you here if I like you."

"What do you want?" he asked.

That little crease formed in the flesh beneath her chin as she tucked it in. "You're so cynical, Rockwall. Were you hurt so many times by women in the past?" She sucked in her breath. "Or so deeply by one?"

"I've been through a few chutes," he told her.

"Then you and I should understand each other," she said. "You won't mention to my uncle about my being with Kenny Graves the other day, will you?"

"Kenny Graves the big flame?"

"Not big enough to burn my fingers." She smiled. "He's just interesting, Rockwall, that's all. The associations around here are so crude. Like Ward." She began running that finger down his collar again, looking up at him. "But now maybe they've smoothed up a bit. One doesn't find an article like you around a corral many times, Rockwall. Put you in a steel pen and Kenny would have to start brushing the straw out of his hair."

"I'd rather not consider myself in competition with him . . . along those lines."

The smile remained, as if she did not know how to take that. Then her eyes had perceived the uncompromising lines of his mouth that would not soften into a smile and her own humor left like an ebbing tide. The light caught opaquely in her narrowing eyes.

"You're so blunt, Rockwall."

"I thought we might as well understand each other from the first," he said. "It's nothing personal. I hope you keep it that way. You're just not my type, that's all. I don't think you're Tie's type, either."

"Big brother?"

"Old friend."

"Same thing."

"And you don't like either?" he asked.

"On the contrary," she purred. "I think it's rather noble of you to look out for his interests so assiduously. Only the boy might have reached the age where he can decide for himself."

"And you're going to let him?"

"Why not?" Her voice was a husky murmur. "He's quite handsome."

"I wouldn't."

"Is that a threat?"

"I never threaten a lady."

"Why don't you?" There was a thin sarcasm in her voice, and she had raised to him slightly. "It would make it so much more exciting. What would you do, Rockwall? Beat me? Take a buggy whip to me? I need some excitement. You're so strong, Rockwall. You might even hurt me. . . ."

"What are you saying?" he asked stiffly.

"I'm wondering if you understand me," she said.

"I don't know," he told her. "Sometimes you glitter. Other times it's like a lamp. Shining and soft."

Her lips formed a half-pleased smile. "When was it like the lamp?"

"When I brought Tie in yesterday. It was good to see."

Her smile faded slightly. "And when did it glitter?"

"When we first met you out in Hellgate Strip. It made you seem older. Harder. It made you seem like one of Graves's girls for sure."

He had not meant to move his eyes, but he found himself glancing unconsciously past her toward the beat-out Appaloosa in the last stall. She caught the glance and interpreted it, and a sudden defiance flashed in her eyes, stiffening her body.

"All right. That's the story. So I was riding last night. I was down at Graves's saloon. But I didn't stay past midnight. It's a long way home."

"It's none of my business," he said.

She stared at him in pouting anger. "Yet you're sitting in judgment on me. I can see it in your eyes. It's ugly."

"I try not to sit in judgment on anybody," he said.

"Then why are you so afraid of me? Every time I come up, you back off like a spooky horse."

"Listen, Aldis," he said, "there's nothing personal in my feelings about you. All I know is I can see there's something going on here that I don't want to get mixed up in."

"Then you *do* understand." She caught his arm,

and the sullen defiance was swept from her face by a tense plea. "Rockwall, my only interest in Graves has been that I thought he could give me something I wanted desperately."

"Like getting out from under your uncle's thumb?"

"If it's that obvious, why do you think I'm so terrible?"

"I told you," he said, "it wasn't you personally. It's the whole thing here."

Her plea seemed to bring her closer, till the swell of her breasts touched him. "When I can't stand it up here any longer, I run to Hellgate. Kenny's not as bad as he sounds. He lets me cry on his shoulder. I thought he was the only man in this country strong enough to buck Uncle Black Jack. Then I saw the way you faced up to Uncle Black Jack yesterday."

"So you'd throw Kenny over for me?"

"It's not like that." Something desperate shook her voice. "Can't you believe me? I just need somebody to turn to, Rockwall, I need somebody so bad."

"Everybody's playing both ends against the middle around here," he said, trying to pull free. "I'm not going to be the one that gets pinched off in between."

"Rockwall," she said. "Please. . . ."

All the glitter was gone now. Her face was left shining and soft like a trusting, pleading child's.

He tried to block off the impulses that rose in him, but he couldn't. He kept remembering the way her room had looked yesterday, barren and unlived-in, kept remembering the way Jennings's face had purpled with rage when she had antagonized him. And she was too close. Rockwall felt his arms stealing about her waist, felt them lift her higher toward him, till those parted lips touched his.

He didn't know how long it lasted. Finally he pulled back, staring at her in a twisted, frustrated way.

"No," he said gutturally. "No." He turned and walked back down the aisle, still trembling.

"What did you say about types . . . Rockwall?"

Chapter Five

The days passed slowly for Rockwall after that. He avoided Aldis as much as possible. Twice more she went down to Hellgate, and after one of these trips he heard the girl and Black Jack quarreling violently in the kitchen. The spring evenings brought the sweet, resinous scent of poplars on a cool wind. The trees stood around the house in a protective cluster, the moon throwing the mottled shadows of their foliage across the flagstones of the long front porch. It was well over a week after they had arrived that Rockwall wandered out after supper to catch a smoke alone before going up to talk with Tie. He liked these moments to himself, when he could look back over the events of the day and the people that had formed them, shifting them back and forth against each other in a study of future possibilities. It was an odd habit of mind, he often reflected, to test the past against the future, when so many were content to let each experience fade so soon behind them. It had been taken for cynicism in him. But a man didn't make the same mistake twice, very often, if he put things together this way.

Rockwall then started walking with the resinous scent of poplars mingling with the reek of dust still holding the heat of the sun. He had almost reached the porch when the boy came out of the door. The curly yellow head was hatless and he had one of Jennings's monogrammed shirts on, too big for him and billowing out around his belt. His arm was still in a sling and he carried it gingerly, grinning at Rockwall.

"Where's Aldis?" Tie greeted him.

"You aren't well enough to be out here yet," Rockwall told him.

"Y'know"—the Texan grinned—"she's right. You're as fussy as an old mother hen."

"You been seeing a lot of her?" Rockwall asked.

"Not half as much as I'd like. She's been a

good nurse. Gets lonely up there in that room."
The boy frowned. "She told me you didn't go for
her. What's the matter, Del?"

"She tell you what smooth edges you have?"

Tie chuckled. "And I gave her all my pet lines.
Why do you let it bother you so, Del? It's always
the same game. Why don't you like her?"

"She's no good for us, Tie."

"You mean for you," said Tie. "Or maybe it's the
other way around. Maybe you like her so much
you're afraid to admit it. Did she kiss you?"

Rockwall did not answer, and Tie nodded. "She
kissed me. Are we in competition, Del?"

"Tie, leave her alone."

The boy was sobering. "We *are* in competition."

"Don't be a fool, Tie. I wouldn't come any
closer to her than I would a snake."

"That's pretty rough talk," said Tie. "If you
really feel that way, Del, don't put it in words
again. I won't take offense now because I guess
you didn't know exactly how I felt. But don't say
anything like that again about her in my presence
or out of it. I want to keep on being friends."

Rockwall stared at the boy, realizing the subtle
change that had occurred. Some of the wild
recklessness was gone from his face. For a
moment, Rockwall glimpsed in its place a flame,
a depth he had not thought Tie capable of.

"No," he said. "I guess I didn't know exactly
how you felt, Tie. I didn't mean Aldis was poison

herself. But she's caught in something here that's poison. Can't you see what's going on, Tie?"

"I never felt this way before, Del."

"Felt what way before?" chortled Black Jack Jennings, coming out of the door with a cut-glass decanter and some tall glasses. "Have some of this, boy, it'll cure everything from gunshot to saddle sores. The finest peach brandy north of Fort Worth. Join us, Rockwall?"

Rockwall stared at the man, trying to understand the change in Jennings's attitude toward the boy. The cane chair *creaked* as he lowered his massive frame into it, leaning forward to pour, and that rich chortle rolled from him again.

"I saw you riding Garnet this afternoon," he told Rockwall. "She's sweet as a baby. That hackamore was a bright idea."

"Baxter's credit," murmured Rockwall.

"Don't fool me." Jennings laughed. "Baxter hasn't got the brains to pull a switch like that. Or the guts. Tie, use your influence on this man. With him as my ramrod, I'd have the best string of horses in Montana."

Tie shook his head. "It's like I told you, Mister Jennings. Rockwall's after a stake of his own. He offered me a part in it. There aren't many ranches around here that work nothing but horses. Most outfits have got their own remudas, like yours, but they're willing to buy choice stuff outside. Our bread and butter would be the wild stuff we sell right out of the trap. They'll bring ten dollars a head. But out of every bunch there's always a couple worth keeping. I'll break them, Del will gentle and polish. A good all-around cow horse will bring fifty to a hundred dollars easy."

Rockwall tasted his brandy, finding it ironic that it should be someone else who was telling Jennings so enthusiastically something that had been the dream of his lifetime. Something was in the making here, and Rockwall still could not put his finger on it. "Yes," he said, "how much would you pay, say, for Tie's steel dust?"

Jennings studied that a moment. "Forty dollars?"

"Forty dollars!" exploded Tie. "That wouldn't pay for one hair from her tail. You've never seen her work. She'll cut a biscuit so thin you don't know it's been pared. She'll chop anything out of a herd from grizzlies to jack rabbits, and . . ."

"All right, all right," conceded Jennings. "I see what you're driving at, Rockwall. A top cow horse will bring a nice price well enough."

"I've seen Quarter animals like Little Billy go for twenty-five hundred dollars down in Texas," said Rockwall. "That kind don't come along often, it's true. But that's only one of the angles. There's a dozen. Our bread and butter would be wild stuff we catch and break. Choppers. Ropers. Night horses. There's always a market. If you won't buy them, your hands will."

"Sounds like a good idea, Rockwall," Jennings said. "I've got one myself. There's a spur of my land, a thousand acres maybe, sticking up into the Garnets. It should be ideal for a horse ranch like you've got in mind. Why don't you use it?"

"What's your price?" Rockwall asked.

"Price?" asked Jennings blandly.

"Blue Boy, maybe?" Rockwall asked.

"Now, Rockwall, don't be like that."

"You wanted to trade your niece for the horse the last time," Rockwall said. "Isn't a thousand acres of land sort of small time compared with that?"

The chair creaked again as Jennings leaned forward sharply. Rockwall saw the hot, puzzled anger fill Tie's eyes, too.

"Look here, Rockwall," Jennings told him in a loud, angry voice. "Don't buck me on that horse. I've got my mind put on having him. If you caught him and wouldn't sell, I'd . . . I'd . . ."

He trailed off, and Rockwall smiled at him. "You'd what, Mister Jennings . . . ?"

Jennings stared into his glass, gripping it tightly in both hands. "I've got a lot of power up here, Rockwall. I could make you or break you."

"I haven't got the horse yet," said Rockwall softly.

"That's right." Jennings's smile came a little forced. "We are putting a cart in front, aren't we?'

Before any of them could speak further, furtive

footsteps sounded in the yard. It was El Potter, his dirty white shirt shining dimly in the twilight. He came halfway up the steps, slouched over in a vaguely defensive way.

"Well, El," Jennings asked impatiently, "what is it?"

"I'm not one to carry a tale, Mister Jennings." The man paused.

"If you've got something to say, say it."

"Well . . ." The man scratched at his matted beard. "It's Saturday night. You know all the hands hit town on Saturday night. . . ."

Again he paused, and Jennings gave him an irritable, verbal push. "I know. It's customary. It's perfectly all right. I've never docked you for getting drunk Saturday night yet, have I, El?"

"Drunk? I was never drunk. You know that, Mister . . ."

"Damn you, El, will you tell me whatever it is!"

The man almost lost his footing on the step. Then he slouched forward, moving down a step, eyes wide. "Well . . . like I say . . . I was in town. Not drunk, mind you. You know I never get drunk. I was in town . . . and . . . and . . . I saw Miss Spain with Kenny Graves!"

The last came in a barely coherent, blurted way, and he cringed as he finished it, half turning as if to go, then halting himself indecisively, like a dog not knowing whether to expect a kick or a reward. Jennings did not move in his chair, or make a sound. The blood slowly filled his face till it was so dark it almost looked Negroid.

There was a startling burst of glass, and a *tinkle* against the flagstones. He looked stupidly at the remnants of the glass he had crushed between his hands. Suddenly he rose, coming up easily and lithely, with none of the grunting effort it had caused him to get his massive frame erect before.

"All right, El," he said, and Rockwall thought there was a tremor in his voice. He turned and went inside. With a glance at Tie, Rockwall followed him. Jennings went past the immense stone fireplace at one end of the long room and through the door of his own bedroom. When he emerged, he had his tweed town coat on, and a stag-butted Bisley stuck nakedly through the middle of his belt.

"You don't have any of your men here," said Rockwall.

"They wouldn't mean much if I did," said Jennings. "Baxter isn't worth much in a tight, Rockwall. You've probably already seen that. I haven't really got one man on the payroll I can trust to back me when the chips are down."

"You can't brace Graves alone."

Jennings stared at him, as if catching the implication. "You?"

"I'm from Texas," Rockwall said.

Jennings laughed unpleasantly. "Whose skin are you more afraid for . . . mine, or my niece's?"

The man had struck home, but Rockwall did not betray it. "Do you want me or not?" he asked.

"Maybe you're not afraid of what might happen to Aldis from Graves," muttered Jennings, squinting at him. "Maybe you're more afraid of what might happen to her from me."

"Go yourself, then," said Rockwall.

Jennings stared at him for what seemed a long time. "You don't have to do this."

"Forget the gratitude," said Rockwall. "I think I'd ride with you whether you had taken Tie in or not."

"And whether you had a score to settle with Graves or not?"

"Yes," said Rockwall. "Do you believe it?"

"I do," said Jennings. "Come on then. No gratitude. No score with Graves. Just a couple of Texas men riding into town. How's that?"

"That's exactly the way it should be." Rockwall grinned. "I've seen more than one town practically demolished on that basis."

Tie was at the door when they went through. "You ain't going without me?"

"You aren't well enough to ride," Rockwall told him.

"Del," pleaded Tie. "I can take a buckboard. You'll let me drive the buckboard, won't you, Black Jack?"

Jennings had to chuckle at this familiarity.

"Rockwall's right, Tie. You aren't fit for it. Better stay here."

"Del!" Tie's voice held a note of hysteria.

Rockwall caught his arm, speaking sharply. "You stay here, understand. If I catch you trying to follow us, I'll knock your ears down, and I'm not joking."

All the way to the stables they could see the boy's forlorn figure silhouetted in the doorway. Jennings saddled up a big sorrel and gave Rockwall his pick, suggesting a claybank in the end stall. Rockwall threw the Menea he'd been working with Garnet onto the claybank and cinched up.

The road into town lay through the cañon used for centuries by the Salish Indians to reach the plains beyond. The Blackfeet had chosen this ideal spot for ambush to massacre so many parties of Salish that the French came to call the place Porte de l'Enfer, or Gate of Hell.

As they rode through bright moonlight to the town road, Jennings slapped his saddle horn disgustedly.

"Serves me right for ever getting mixed up with that hellion in the first place."

"How did she come under your wing?" Rockwall asked.

"Aldis's mother was my sister," Jennings said. "She married a tinhorn gambler in Louisiana. My sister died when Aldis was born. The girl grew up a cardsharp's daughter, living high one day, low the next. That's what makes her so hard."

"Maybe you haven't given her a chance," Rockwall said.

"Chance?" Jennings shook his head viciously. "Give her an inch and she takes a mile. Her father died years ago, sent her up here for me to take care of till she was of age. She and I haven't got along from the first day. Nothing I can do will bring her to heel. It seems she gets wilder every day. Times like this I want to take a horsewhip to her."

Rockwall was unable to block the anger thickening his throat at this. It made him realize how much the girl had motivated his coming with Jennings, drawing him to her even though he knew it might very well kick back at him later on. He had the sense of being sucked in by something over which he had no control.

It made him think of the blue roan. He'd had the same feeling at his first sight of Blue Boy. He had been sucked in by it. *Were the girl and the horse that much alike? Outlaws, untamed, so beautiful in spirit and flesh a man couldn't keep away from them?* He shook his head savagely, trying to rid himself of this pointless introspection.

The town itself lay on the flat bed of a prehistoric lake, spreading out in a haphazard flow of frame buildings toward the towering Sapphires to the south. They crossed the Higgins Avenue bridge and turned up Cammas Street.

This was lined with false-fronted saloons filled with all the noise and movement of a Saturday night in a cow town. Jennings swung off his sorrel before the gingerbread façade with the big sign advertising the Sapphire Saloon.

"I've tried to keep a check rein on Aldis," he told Rockwall, stepping onto the high wooden curb, "but she's wilder'n a broomtail. Graves is her latest trick like I told you. Nothing I can seem to do will keep her away from him. I warned her the next time she saw him I'd come and get her myself. I can't have a kid like her hanging around Cammas Street. Nobody can stay decent very long down here."

They were inside by the time he had finished muttering this, with the batwing doors flapping behind them, a creaking obbligato to the murmur of voices and *clink* of glassware. It was no different than the countless other saloons Rockwall had been in, and he had been in this one before. The display of purple drapes and gold-filigreed mirrors behind the long mahogany bar had a tawdry effect. On the other side of the room, a bored croupier was spinning a roulette wheel. Rockwall saw Ward Baxter in the crowd about the table. He took one look at Jennings, and then shifted behind someone else.

There were other small movements in the room that Rockwall did not miss. Tony Laroque appeared abruptly from a knot of men near the end of the bar, a half-filled glass in one hand, and started moving sideways toward the rear. In the group around a poker table behind the roulette layout, a man, catching Laroque's eye, removed a cigarette from his mouth, flicking it at a brass spittoon in a corner, and started shifting unobtrusively toward the back. Jennings saw Rockwall's attention on him and muttered: "George Stanak. Mixed up with Graves's gambling interests, somehow. You want to watch for a knife."

Everything about Stanak reminded Rockwall of a knife. The creases in his broadcloth coat and foxed trousers were like blade edges. His face was sharp, pointed, without expression, save for the eyes, glittering with some congenital malevolence from beneath eyelids like hoods. Both Laroque and Stanak were slightly ahead of Rockwall and Jennings. Jennings saw Rockwall's attention, this time on the door at the rear, and once more interpreted the look.

"That opens into a hall," he told Rockwall. "Three short card rooms on the right, three offices on the left. Graves has the middle office."

"What say we reach him first?" said Rockwall.

"The jump is always the advantage." Jennings smiled.

The door back there opened outward, and a possibility occurred to Rockwall. It would take a delicate judge of distance and movement. There was a space between the curtain and the wall that Laroque would have to negotiate, coming as he did from over nearer the bar. As the man passed behind this curtain from the end of the bar, momentarily out of sight, Rockwall shifted from his casual deliberate walk into a long stride.

Laroque was just coming from behind the curtain, hand outstretched for the door handle, when Rockwall veered around this side of the hanging, reaching the handle a moment before the man. He pulled the door open as hard as he could. Laroque walked right into the opening edge with his face.

"My God," said Rockwall. "I didn't see you coming."

"You got a deuce," said Jennings softly from behind, and Rockwall wheeled to see Stanak almost upon them, with the flash of a knife blade appearing from his sleeve. Before the hilt of it was completely in his palm, however, Rockwall had taken the one long step necessary to reach the man, jamming his left arm in between Stanak's right arm and body until their elbows were hooked. Jennings took the cue beautifully, doing the same thing from the other side. Together they walked the man right back into the wall. He struck so hard the whole structure shuddered, and Rockwall saw his eyes bulge out with the impact. While the man's body was still stiffened with shock against the wall, Rockwall yanked the knife from his limp fingers and gave it a casual flip that stuck it in the ceiling five feet above their heads.

"Well, damn it."' Jennings laughed. "You really are from Texas."

Rockwall grasped Stanak by the collar, banging his head back against the wall. "Say something. Quick."

"What?" asked Stanak dazedly, feebly trying to squirm free. His voice was high, womanish, shrill. "What?"

"Nothing," growled Rockwall, and let him slump backward, turning toward the door.

"You looking for the man with the frog voice?" asked Jennings.

"I'll find him," said Rockwall.

They passed through the door with Laroque still huddled over beyond, holding his bleeding face. Jennings halted an instant to listen before that middle door on the right side. There was murmuring talk and the muted slap of cards from the rooms across the hall, but none from within here. Jennings threw the door wide without stepping in.

There was a cheap print of Goya's nude Duchess over a scarred Chippendale desk, and inch-deep nap to the carpet extending to the walls. There was the scent of expensive whiskey and a faint hint of perfume in the air. But no one was in the room. Then, from one of the doors on the other side of the passage, a woman's laugh, throaty and seductive. There was something vaguely tortured in the look Jennings tossed at Rockwall. Then, the effort of will plainly in his face, he moved across and opened that door.

Rockwall had that glimpse of them within before they had recovered from surprise. The two older men should have been at a chamber of commerce meeting. One was balding and with a cold cigar. The other had iron-gray hair, and a belly as substantial as his standing in the community probably was. There was a young man who had removed his coat to reveal fancy galluses and a loud shirt, and there was a fourth, sallow-faced player with the long, sensitive hands of a professional card player. Aldis was dealing, with her back to the door, but she had turned to see who was there. Her gown had no back. The bright light of two round-bowled china lamps turned the bare flesh of the girl's shoulders to tinted alabaster and made rich wine of the crimson moiré covering her deep breasts as she turned to see who had entered. Anger narrowed her eyes, making them look much older. Her plucked brows raised faintly as she recognized Jennings, and there was that blasé indulgence to her voice as she spoke to him.

"Well, Uncle, come for a little game?"

Jennings fists were clenched at his sides, and his voice held a guttural tremor. "You know why I've come, Aldis. Get your wrap. Your coming back to the Forked Tongue with me."

Graves must have been standing to the girl's right, and the opening door had blocked him off that long. But now he shoved it against the wall to give him room between table and door. He had no coat on, and it gave Rockwall a new idea of the man. Most people followed the usual fallacies in judging strength, impressed by the narrow hips or the broad square shoulders or the big bicep. Graves's shoulders were not noticeably broad. In fact, with relation to his thick, square waist, they looked almost narrow. But the swinging motion of his body drew the white shirt, for an instant, across the swelling outline of a deltoid, and caused the cloth to ripple with the thick surge of muscle from shoulder to neck that made it difficult to button his outsize collar.

"Well," he said, looking at Rockwall. "Think you'd find some horses in here?"

"I wouldn't be surprised," said Rockwall.

The momentary shift of focus in Graves's eyes might have indicated an attempt to read Rockwall's enigmatic face. Then the man was looking at Jennings. "Riding the horse pretty hard, aren't you, Black Jack, when you come into other people's establishments and order them around?"

Jennings's effort to control himself was painfully apparent. "Don't block me, Graves. Don't do anything. Just stay right where you are and let my niece get up and come with me."

The girl's whole body seemed to rise up a little.

In the glow of her cheeks Rockwall could see a deep defiance. There was an instant of silence before she spoke. It gave Rockwall time to notice the underarm harness lying on a side table near Kenny Graves. The grips of a Colt house gun protruded sullenly from the holster.

"I'm not coming with you, Uncle," Aldis said then. "You might as well go."

All of Jennings's restraint seemed to shatter with his wild roar. He lunged violently into the room, one arm lifted as though to strike the girl. Graves jumped toward him, trying to stop him. Jennings caught the man by the shoulder, spinning him backward. Graves crashed into the side table, almost turning it over.

Jennings grabbed the girl's arm, yanking her brutally out of the chair. Graves caught his balance, pulling at the house gun holstered on the table.

"You're too late, Graves," Rockwall said.

All the others had been jumping to their feet, kicking their chairs back, shouting. Rockwall's voice stopped this as sharply as it stopped Graves. There was a moment empty of sounds as they stared at the gun in Rockwall's hand.

At that moment, Laroque came down the hall in a stumbling, uncertain walk, a blood-soaked handkerchief held to his nose. "I tried to stop them, Kenny," he mumbled. "They looked like they was coming through, and I tried . . ." He halted and backed up against the wall, staring at Rockwall's gun, too.

"Never mind, Tony," said Graves. "There won't be any trouble, I'm sure." The light glittered in the vivid intelligence of his eyes, regarding Jennings. "I think it's about time you stopped playing god, Jennings. Your niece is of age now. If she wants to come to my place, that's her business."

Suddenly Aldis began struggling violently in Jennings's grip. "Let me go, Black Jack, I'm of age now, damn you. I can go wherever I want to, let go . . . !"

"Quit it, damn you!" Jennings shouted.

Rockwall saw the man's fingers tighten on her arm. She doubled forward, face twisting with pain, still fighting. Jennings slapped her brutally across the face with his palm, then hit her again, backhand. Her head rocked so hard she almost jerked out of Jennings's grasp. Rockwall stepped impulsively toward Jennings, hot with anger. But he saw Graves move as soon as he did, and had to stop. To fight with Jennings now would weaken their front against Graves and his men and leave them in too dangerous a position.

Aldis's eyes were glassy with shock and she jerked like a puppet as Jennings swung her around, pushing her through the door. Trembling with his restraint, Rockwall jerked his gun for Graves to follow. The man moved across in front of him, face stiff with anger.

"You're a fool, Rockwall," said Graves. "You won't get out of here alive."

"Maybe if you go in front of me, your muscle men won't be so eager to use their deweys on me," said Rockwall, flicking the tip of his gun for Graves to keep moving. The man did not react, staring at Rockwall in anger. "Maybe you'd like me to use my dewey on you," said Rockwall, moving the gun again.

Graves took a deep breath, and stepped into the hall, following Jennings. Rockwall indicated Laroque should do the same, and moved in behind the two men as they went to the end of the hall.

There was a subdued murmur to the sound of the crowd outside. Jennings moved fast and so did Graves. Rockwall had to speed up to keep close. He left the hall door, expecting Stanak to be just beyond, but the man was not there. Graves passed the curtain that hung to one side of the door, and his head turned in a small jerk to the right. He moved his head back as if trying to hide the motion, but Rockwall had not missed it. He saw Stanak now, about ten feet to the right of the hanging.

Rockwall's attention was shifting back to Graves, and he was just passing the curtain when it happened. He wheeled, with the sense of having missed something by looking at Stanak, but before he was around far enough to see it, the hand came from back of the curtain in an arc, with ten inches of loaded pool cue in it. It struck his gun arm.

Sound left him in a rended gust. He felt the gun slip from fingers stiffening with pain that burned. He saw Graves swinging around. He saw the bartender lunge from back of the drapes, raising the pool cue for another blow.

Rockwall threw himself bodily at the man's knees. It was the only way he could have evaded the blow. He felt his body jackknife about the man's legs and they went into the curtain, pulling it off with them as they tumbled in a heap to the floor. Rockwall got his good hand on the loaded club and jerked it free of the bartender's grip. The man tried to grapple him, and Rockwall hit him in the face with it.

Free to rise, he had not yet gotten off his knees when the arm holding the sawed-off pool cue was hooked through the elbow from behind. He whirled violently to keep from having it thrown into a hammerlock, and his face came around into Graves's solid belly. He saw how it was now. There was a vicious, personal vindication in the way Graves tore the pool cue from his hands.

Rockwall saw it coming, and tried to block Graves's arm. But the man brought the blow up from below. The loaded end of the cue made a *crunching* sound against Rockwall's wrist, tearing it aside to strike his chin. The heavy, upward blow lifted him off the floor, knocking him back between the bar and the back wall.

He felt his feet doing a crazy shuffle beneath him in an effort to keep from falling. His outflung arm swept a whole row of bottles off the shelf as he staggered backward. Liquor formed a slippery pool beneath his boots, and he slipped on the broken glass, and fell at last, halfway down the bar.

His jaw felt immensely swollen, and a pulse of pain beat through it like a drum. He tried to grab hold of something and pull himself erect, but the space between the bar and the shelves was so narrow he could get no purchase. He rolled over on his belly and came to his hands and knees. Behind him he could hear a foot crash into the first of that broken glass, and knew that was Graves, and it left him only another second.

Desperately he reached his right hand up to grab the bar and pull himself erect and whirl all at once. He had not gotten his head above the level of the bar when George Stanak appeared at the other end of the narrow passageway, another knife in his hand. Rockwall heard his breath erupt in a gasp of complete understanding as he whirled the other way to see Graves right on top of him, the pool cue upraised. An awesome sense of utter helplessness robbed him of will in that last moment, still crouched in that cramped position, caught between the two of them.

"Both of you jaspers better stop right there,"

said a soft, drawling voice from somewhere beyond the bar, "unless you want to see just how hot the lead from Texas is."

The glass made a gritty, crunching sound beneath Graves's boots as his weight settled with the complete cessation of movement. Stanak halted himself a foot from Rockwall, the knife reflecting light in a wicked flash. Rockwall lifted himself up to a standing position, hands on the bar top, and then he could see, too. Tie Taylor stood just inside the front door of the saloon, and the Bisley in his hand looked like a cannon to Rockwall.

"Fort Worth sends a little help." Tie grinned

Chapter Six

June was the month for rain. It came heavily that night after they got home from Hellgate, and stopped before morning, to let the rising sun draw gray serpents of steam out of the buffalo grass and glitter brazenly on the poplar leaves around the Forked Tongue ranch house. Jennings had spoken of wanting to see Garnet perform, and Rockwall went down early to bit up the horse and bring her back through monkey grass gleaming like wet blood. He found Tie and Aldis coming out the front door with the older man behind, a hand on each shoulder, a grin on his weathered face.

"You're the second to congratulate them, Rockwall!" Jennings shouted.

Something cold and sick settled in Rockwall's stomach. "For what?"

"For getting married," Tie told him.

"Oh." Rockwall let his eyes meet the girl's for a moment. Her smile had been easy, but it stiffened into something fixed. The corner of her lip twitched faintly with the tension of drawn muscle. Then Rockwall moved his gaze to Jennings. "You like the idea?"

"Like it?" roared Jennings. "The boy's from Texas, isn't he? Got more guts than you can hang on a fence, hasn't he? Coming in with that buckboard last night to pull us all out of a tight when nine out of ten would have gone back to bed with that wound. You bet I like it. I like it so much I'm giving them that thousand acres up in the Garnets for a wedding present." He dropped his hands from their shoulders, coming between them to walk down the steps and put a hand on Rockwall's knee.

"There's a condition to it, though, Rockwall. I make the land a gift to all three of you, in reality. I know Tie's been in on that dream of yours about raising horses. But he isn't experienced enough to make a go of it alone. I'm giving them that thousand acres on the condition that you go in as a partner. You'll have your horse ranch, Tie gets Aldis."

Rockwall found his eyes on the girl's face again, and his head making a negative motion. "I . . . I couldn't do that, Mister Jennings."

"Couldn't?" Jennings whole face twisted in the effort to understand this as he withdrew his hand. "Why not? It's the chance you've been wanting all your life. Both of you. You'll have all the help I can give you, Rockwall, you know that."

Rockwall shook his head again. "No. It just wouldn't work out. If they marry"—he found something blocking his throat, and had to clear it—"if they marry, they'll want to be alone. You can't tie another man to it from the start that way. It's their outfit, wagon and team. They won't want somebody else tagging along. . . ."

"You won't be second fiddle," said Jennings. "It'll be yours as much as theirs, Rockwall. I told you. Partners. Naturally I make it a gift and you're in on it."

Rockwall studied him a moment, then said dryly: "What does Aldis get?"

Jennings frowned at him in puzzled anger. "She gets Tie. What the hell are you quibbling about? How many men get a chance at half ownership of land like that for nothing?"

"Or for a blue roan?" Rockwall said.

Tie frowned at Rockwall. "What are you driving at?"

"This," Rockwall said. "How long do you think it will take to prove to Mister Jennings you can handle this set-up on your own? Six months? A year?" He turned to Jennings. "And by that time, maybe, we'll have caught the roan?"

"Maybe," said Jennings.

"And if we haven't got the roan . . . does the marriage still go on?"

"Del," Tie said, "you're making it sound like the marriage, the whole thing, depends on that roan." He stared at Rockwall, as if waiting for an answer. When he got none, the boy looked at Jennings. "You haven't answered Rockwall's question yet. What if we don't get the roan?"

Jennings was too blunt a man to carry it off. The geniality was too slow in filling his face, and came with palpable effort. His chuckle was brassy and false.

"Now, Tie, you know what a suspicious varmint your sidekick here is. Don't let him put any false notions in your head."

Tie was still frowning, his face sullen with youthful anger. Rockwall could see that he was beginning to understand how Jennings was using him. Then the boy was turning to Aldis, with the expression changing in his face. The anger remained, but it was more bewildered now. And in his eyes shone a poignant desire. Rockwall

75

realized that, even if Tie saw how he was being used, the spell Aldis exerted on him would make him trade his pride for her. Rockwall knew a savage desire to prevent that.

Tie might think he could trade it now and not suffer. Rockwall knew better. A man was nothing without his self-respect. Rockwall had seen too many men who had lost it somewhere along the way. Then Rockwall found his eyes moving to the girl. The deep, frightened plea in her eyes shook his resolve. She wanted this, he realized, even more than Tie. Either way he turned, he would let one of them down. He shook his head.

"That's it, that's it." A suppressed desperation had entered Rockwall's voice. "You can't tie another man in on a wedding present that way. It would be like sending the best man along on the honeymoon."

"Surely your friendship is strong enough to overcome an idea like that. It's the very reason I made the offer. I thought you and Tie were close enough to accept something like it." Jennings lowered his voice confidentially. "I didn't make all my judgment on the boy himself, Rockwall, as much as I think of him. A man's friends tell a lot about him. I'd consider myself fortunate to have a friend like you."

"Thanks, Mister Jennings," said Rockwall through stiff lips. "But I can't . . . I can't . . ."

Jennings stepped back. "I'm disappointed in

you, Rockwall. Perhaps your friendship for the boy isn't as strong as I thought. Maybe I wouldn't be so fortunate at that."

Rockwall knew the torture in him showed in his face as he stared at Jennings. He had a terrible impulse to answer, to try and explain; he blocked it with a great effort, knowing how inexplicable, how nebulous his motives were in this. Yet they were so valid for him, so poignant, that they caused him an actual, physical pain, as he turned his eyes up for a moment to Tie. He did not speak when their glances met, but it was all in his eyes.

Rockwall wheeled the horse and trotted her back down to the barn. Baxter was within the building, stretching and yawning.

"How'd Jennings like her?" he asked.

Rockwall swung off without answering, and started to move away.

"What's the matter, did she act up?" asked the man. The vague triumph in his voice caused Rockwall to turn part way back, letting the words out savagely.

"You know she didn't. She'll be all right if you don't rein her like you were digging a ditch."

"I told you that hackamore wouldn't work," said Baxter.

Rockwall wanted to hit the man. But he made himself walk out of the barn and down to the poplar grove, where a trickle of a creek ran through the cat-tails. Finding a sandy bank, he sat down and rolled a cigarette in the greatest defeat he had felt in many years. A magpie made its black and white flash through the larch, and began scolding at him. He hardly heard the bird. The whispering of the cat-tails made no more impression on him. Then Aldis came out of the trees. She stood above him, looking at his face.

"You're not going through with it, are you?" she said at last. "I never expected to see you sulking."

"Let it go, will you?" he said. "I don't want to talk."

"It was you who kissed me, if you'll remember," she said. "All I asked for was your help. If it got out of hand, who's to blame? I guess you realize how deeply you've hurt Tie."

He ground his cigarette out, staring up at her with a deep frown. "I think he knew how I'd react."

"I never told him I loved him." It seemed an effort for her to speak. "I told him I was fond of him. When he asked me to marry him, I made it plain that I didn't love him the way he loves me. He has hopes that I'll grow to love him. I don't know about that. I only know that I was perfectly honest with Tie. You can ask him."

He rose slowly, shaken by this, staring at her. "I thought I realized before how badly you wanted to escape your uncle. But"—he held out his hand helplessly—"you'd be willing to marry a man you don't love . . . ?"

"Why not?" Her chin raised, eyes flashing. "Can't you understand that? Can't you see what it's like, living under Black Jack's thumb . . . ?" She broke off, settling back. The flame left her eyes. When she spoke again, her voice was dull and brittle. "No. Of course, you can't. You can't begin to know what it's like to have him try to break you like he breaks his horses. To have him keep you on a leash like you were a dog and take his fist to you like a dog when you can't stand it any more and try to escape. I won't try to tell you how many times I tried to run away. He came after me every time. Halfway around the world wouldn't be far enough . . ." Her voice had risen with each word, until it was high and intense when she finally broke off once more, seeking some sign of sympathy in his face.

He could not help showing it, and yet he still retained his wariness.

"You really hate me, don't you?" she said then. "Why, Rockwall?"

His gaze was utterly uncompromising. "Maybe I understand you."

Her eyes flashed. "What do you understand of me?"

"A lot of things. What happens to Kenny Graves?"

"I told you what he meant to me," she said. "He was only a means of temporary escape. He asked me to marry him. It would have been useless.

You saw Uncle Black Jack come after me last night. Graves wasn't strong enough to buck him. The only way Graves could have done it was with the blue roan. I don't doubt Uncle Black Jack would have made a deal with him. He'll get along. What was I supposed to do? Twiddle my thumbs in a garret till Tie came along? I liked Kenny. I admit it."

"The way you like me?"

Little lines appeared at the corners of her squinting eyes, as she bent toward him. "I thought maybe that was it. Maybe it isn't that you dislike me so much. Maybe you like me too much. Maybe you're afraid to come along with Tie and me."

He stared up at her, and for a moment that intense attraction he had felt when they had kissed filled him, for a moment the possibility occurred to him that she was right. Then the betrayal of that—of feeling something like that for the betrothed of his best friend—became plain to him, and he denied it to himself in a vicious, savage way. But to her, he raised his eyes, asking: "What do you think?"

She studied his face narrowly, shrugging finally. "I don't know what to think, Rockwall. I only wish you'd give me some kind of chance. Do you think it utterly impossible for me to love someone? It isn't as if this happened overnight. I've seen Tie almost every day for some time now."

"And you were at Graves's last night."

A dogged look entered her face. "Black Jack and I had a fight. I had to do something." She bent toward him, a new, tense tone to her voice. "You say you understand me. How can you? How can you know what it is to be sent to finishing school when you hated it, shipped back East for college when your whole life was here, kept on a check rein so tight it hurt from the minute you got back, told what to wear, who to see, when to get up, what to eat, until you thought you'd go crazy. Sure I broke over the traces. So would you. Sure I sought excitement. Tell me you wouldn't. If you're so proud of all your precise little judgments on life, if you're so sure you understand me, then try to really understand me. I have the same longings as you. I think they're as decent as yours. I want someone decent to love, a home, kids. I always have."

Her passionate intensity reached a sympathy in him he had not thought existed. He stared into her face, trying to believe fully what he was hearing. She brought her face so near his the heat of her breath struck him, and she gripped his shoulder.

"Give me a chance, at least, Rockwall, give us both a chance, Tie and me. You didn't come all this way with Tie to let him down when he needs you most. He can't make out with that horse ranch on his own, you know he can't. If I wasn't in the picture, you would have jumped at the chance. There isn't any reason why you and I can't get along, Rockwall. We just started out on the wrong foot, that's all. Let's forget Kenny Graves and that scene in the barn and everything else, let's start over again, for Tie's sake. I'll stay out of your way."

It shook his faith in his own judgment that he had not seen this side in Aldis before; it almost hurt him. He felt awkward before her now, an awkwardness he had not known before a woman since he was a kid, dating his first girl. There was something clean about it, refreshing. He knew if he could maintain the feeling in her presence, what she wanted would be possible.

"Tie's waiting on the porch," she said.

For a last instant he tried to look at it objectively. He had been given the feeling that he would sell Tie out by accepting Black Jack's proposition and letting the boy sacrifice his pride for want of Aldis. Now he had the same feeling about the girl—that he would be selling Aldis out if he refused to help her escape Jennings. Somehow he could see neither course as good. It only seemed the lesser of two evils to give in now. He nodded slowly, seeing the radiant triumph in her face, and together they walked back to the house.

Tie rose from Black Jack's big armchair as he saw them coming up the knoll. Jennings himself was not in sight.

"Still want that partner?" Rockwall asked.

Tie stared at him, comprehension slowly dawning in his face, flushing it. Finally he let out a whoop. "Do I! Boy, howdy! You really mean it, Del?"

"How about riding up to take a look at your land?" said Rockwall.

"Our land!" shouted Tie, running down the steps. "Our land!"

Seeing the happiness shining in both their eyes, Rockwall felt himself swept up by the jubilance of the moment. Maybe it was right after all, he thought. It had to be right.

Chapter Seven

Rockwall built the house that June, while Tie and Aldis spent their honeymoon in one of Jennings's mountain lodges high in the Sapphires. Jennings put all his resources at Rockwall's command, sending laborers and carpenters up from Hellgate, shipping finished lumber from his own Black Jack Mills in town. Tie and Rockwall had chosen the site, set on a southern slope to be protected from the northern winds, surrounded by timber, overlooking a gurgling mountain stream.

The foundation was of great round niggerheads

taken from the mountains themselves and cemented with grout. The outer walls were of undressed pine logs, and the inside of finished lumber from the mills, with pegged hardwood floors and a stone fireplace in each room. The place was furnished and the great hip-roofed barn and half a dozen corrals were finished by the time Tie returned with his bride.

It was near the end of August by then, and Rockwall wanted to start running down some wild bunches to have working stock before winter set in. Reluctantly Tie took leave of Aldis for the first trip into Hellgate Strip. The cottonwoods were turning yellow along the cutbanks and the plumes of the bear grass were getting ragged. It took the men two days to flush a bunch and another day to trap them. They culled out, and had four decent possibilities to bring back. Tie started topping them right away to give Rockwall a couple of gentled animals to work with. One broke his leg bucking, and there was another incorrigible, which left them two broken animals when it was over. With these working in the hackamore, the two men took a run into the Strip again.

By tacit agreement they kept working over toward the southwestern portion of the badlands in hope of sighting Blue Boy. On their fourth trip across Clark Fork and right up against the Sapphires, they finally caught sight of the roan and his band.

They topped a ridge of rock that overlooked a broad sweep of meadow, still grassed-over in patches for the animals to feed, when Tie exclaimed and pointed to them. There must have been a dozen of them, shifting constantly with that unrelieved restlessness of wild things, and Tie and Rockwall immediately dismounted, pulling their animals out of sight to stare in growing excitement. Bays, browns, duns, and pintos. Mares and colts and stallions. And the blue one. The blue roan, with the great muscles of its Quarter blood rippling like snakes and bunching like fists in its rump, and the thick, heavy neck of its Morgan blood arched proudly above the buffalo grass.

For a moment they stared in fascination at the beast. He was not a hot blood. He was not in any stud book. He was not an Arab, with his blood-lines traced back 1,000 years, or a thoroughbred, sired from a great racing stallion. He was a mustang, without brand, without record of his progenitors. He would have chewed a blue ribbon to pulp. He would have pawed a show ring to furrows. Yet he was the kind of horse a cowman would give his soul for.

"I could crease him from here," said Tie in an awed, whispering way.

"And take nine chances out of ten on killing him or ruining him for good," muttered Rockwall. "No, thanks. I've seen too many creased horses. We had an old mare that couldn't lift her head above her hocks because some playboy thought he'd just crease her neck." His brow was knotted, as he spoke, studying the land down there. "If this roan is so hard to nail, he must have some special tricks to keep out of the corral. Let's flush him now. I want to find out how he runs. You circle around and plant three or four spooks." He pointed to a rise across the valley. "Make a line for him toward that ridge. There's benches west of it that he shouldn't try, and that creek eastward is too rough to cross. We'll push him into the ridge till it's the only logical place. Got it?"

"I know what you want." Tie nodded.

"One shot when you're ready," said Rockwall. "Then I'll flush them."

Tie took a last look and went for his horse. The sun was rising toward noon, shortening the shadows in the valley. The roan began to drift, and the bunch to follow him.

They crossed a flat and headed toward a stand of aspens that formed a tightly massed wedge that broke the meadow in half. Rockwall saw Tie's spook about the same time the blue roan did. It was the boy's chaps, thrown across a serviceberry bush at the point of that wedge. They were planted so that they would have turned an ordinary wild one to the left, the direction Rockwall wanted to drive the band. Nine out of ten wild ones would have taken that course, for the trees petered out on that left flank till it was comparatively open, while they grew so densely on the right that a horse would have trouble getting through.

The roan tossed his magnificent head with the first man smell. There was a moment's hesitation. Rockwall could almost see the perverse devil flash in the animal's eyes. Then he turned right. Blue Boy led the band down the edge of timber there, hunting an opening.

Then the shot came, flat and warped by distance, and Rockwall knew it was Tie's signal. He mounted and dropped down into the open slope. The roan saw him and started moving down the valley. Rockwall cut around on the horses' right flanks until he had them traveling in the direction he wanted. Rockwall crowded them till they went headlong through the dense underbrush, scraping hide off on tree trunks, squealing angrily. On the boulder-strewn banks of the stream beyond, he had to maneuver for fifteen minutes before he could get them headed back the way he wanted.

Once again they came to one of Tie's spooks, planted so that an ordinary horse would have been turned in the direction the men wanted to drive the band. And once again the roan turned in the opposite direction, choosing the alternative no normal wild horse would have taken.

Rockwall dismounted, easing his animal's girth, and turned his eyes onto the roan down there, drinking in the magnificence of him the way only a true horseman could. The roan began to drift, and the bunch to follow him, and Rockwall tightened his girth again, in a nervous impatience. The roan was wary now, moving fast, and Rockwall knew the big push would have to come before he lost control over them completely. In all his experience at horse running, he had not yet seen a wild band that wouldn't run a ridge down its full length if given half a chance.

The roan's head lifted sharply. One of the mares whinnied. Rockwall stepped up and dropped down through the spruce and juniper into the open slope of the meadow. The roan saw him and started moving down the valley. Rockwall cut around fast onto their flank in an effort to change their direction and force them directly across. The roan fought it, but Rockwall finally had them traveling toward the stand of aspens fringing the meadow.

The aspens marched into the meadow in a tightly massed wedge that would have logically turned a moving animal to one side or the other. Down the right flank of this wedge for several hundred yards, the trees and underbrush were just as thick, but to the left of the point the trees petered out into a boulder-strewn streambed that had long been dry. Nine wild ones out of ten would have been turned by the point of the wedge onto that comparatively open left flank.

Rockwall followed them, fighting the brush clear through, until they had broken into the dry streambed. Again he got onto their flank, and after ten minutes of maneuvering, had them going in the direction he wanted. They clambered up over a deep, crumbling cutbank and headed across a sand flat toward the benchlands. Rockwall could not help a smile of admiration for Tie, with sight of the third spook. It was the boy's yellow slicker thrown over a boulder. On one side, the sand flat dropped off into a broad gully, and on the other it became a slope of shale and talus so slippery a rider would have a battle driving his mount across it. And again, with that snorting toss of the head, Blue Boy chose the illogical avenue, veering away into that shale slope.

Rockwall had to use his spurs to follow, slipping and sliding down through the broken crust, the horse squealing in equine anger at such stupidity. Another fifteen minutes were spent in maneuvering the band of wild ones back into the line he wanted.   Ahead was the ridge he had pointed out to Tie. The approach was across a broad plateau that was really no more than a great bench formed by a high cliff on one side and a steep slope on the other that dropped down to a boulder-strewn stream. The ridge extended from this plateau, one side dropping off into the same type of benchlands, each tier too steep for a horse to negotiate without a high jump, the other side falling into the same rocky creekbed. There were still some deep pools in the creek, but summer had dried it up so that in most parts the rocks thrust up, through the swirling white water, forming a crossing hated by horses. The ridge itself was the only logical avenue off the plateau.

Rockwall worked the band up onto the plateau, and got them headed toward the other end, and then spurred his horse with a wild whoop. At the same time, Tie came up out of the benches on the left flank of the ridge, where he had been hiding, and he was yelling his head off.

For a moment, with what was almost a disappointment, Rockwall thought it would drive the roan onto the ridge. Then Blue Boy veered off onto the slope toward the vicious roar of tumbling water. Tie and Rockwall pulled up on the highlands, watching the band slip and slide down the steep bank, squealing and whinnying in a maddened chorus as they clattered in through the hated boulders. The roan led them unerringly into deep water, and the band climbed in a dripping, neighing file onto the opposite bank. The roan rounded them up and sent them packing, and then turned in a prancing, snorting way, to lift his head and let out a pealing, triumphant whinny.

"You blue devil," Rockwall murmured with a grin.

"Has he been jumping the wrong way at every spook?" asked Tie, mopping his brow.

"Every one," said Rockwall. "No wonder he's so hard to catch. I never saw a broomtail so man-wise. It's like he sat in on our palaver and learned how we figured to turn him every time, and turned exactly the opposite way when he came to it."

"Del." Something in Tie's voice made Rockwall turn sharply toward him, and then follow the direction of his eyes. "One of those nags didn't get across?"

"They're all on the other side," said Rockwall.

"Then we better duck this skylight here. Somebody's down there. . . ."

The crash of a gun took Rockwall back to that night out in the Strip. There was the scream of a ricochet and shale kicked up a foot from his animal's forehoofs. The horse whinnied shrilly, rearing up. The shale had been kicked down the slope by the bullet. That meant it could not have come from below.

"They're above us, too!" shouted Rockwall, fighting the plunging animal. "Let's dive for the timber down there! It's the only cover!"

He hooked the bay with his spurs and the animal went onto its rump sliding down the steep bank. Another gun crashed from the trees below, and Tie's steel dust lost its footing. Rockwall couldn't tell whether it had been hit or not, but Tie kicked free, and both animal and man went rolling on down the bank. Rockwall managed to keep his horse upright till they hit the water. The horse fought like a crazy tightrope walker to keep its footing among the rocks, its own impetus carrying the beast on forward through the shallows, slipping and sliding, sparks flying from its clattering shoes. Rockwall was afraid to jump with those boulders thrusting their ugly round heads from the water on either side, but the inevitable happened, with the mount screaming as it finally lost footing and went down, plunging the man over its head.

He had a dim impression of round boulders flashing beneath him. When he struck, however, there was nothing but the slap of water against his body, opening, chill and dark, to let him plummet in. His face scraped sandy bottom and he got his feet on it and shoved up. Coming to the surface, he could see that the horse had pitched him into a deep pool.

White water made its roaring foam all about him, and through its snowy curtain he caught sight of the horse, apparently unhurt, as it scrambled erect in the shallows and turned to find its slipping, sliding way back to shore. This deep part was still swept with current, and it was carrying Rockwall down toward more rocks. He paddled himself in a wild, wheeling motion, seeking some way out, but the opposite bank was a sheer side of granite. All he could do was let the current carry him through this deep part, battered this way and that against the rocks till his shirt was torn off and his torso was bloody to the waist.

Finally he reached a place shallow enough for footing, and fought ashore. He crawled out of the water on hands and knees, seeing that he had been swept downstream several hundred yards. Timber extended from here to within a few yards of where Tie lay out on the exposed bank where they had first lost their horses.

At first, Rockwall thought the boy was unconscious. Then he saw that Tie was sprawled on his belly with his Bisley in one hand peering over the top of the rocks at the plateau above. Even as Rockwall watched, a gun hammered from up there, and granite chipped off the rock above Tie's ducking head.

Reaching the sandy shore, Rockwall collapsed, unable to force himself farther for the next few moments. He lay on his belly until he felt enough strength return to lift himself up. His head rose above the cutbank so that he could see Tie once more, upstream. Then Tony Laroque appeared, twenty feet in front of Rockwall. The man had not seen Rockwall, lying beneath that cutbank, and had passed him, pacing toward Tie, a Ward-Burton in his hands. But the motion of Rockwall's rising body caught his attention. He whirled back.

That instant probably saved Rockwall's life for he had already begun pulling his own gun free. As Laroque started to jerk the rifle into line, Rockwall squeezed the trigger. It made a dank, metallic *click* against the wet brass of the cartridge.

With the black bore of Laroque's Ward-Burton pointed right at him, Rockwall squeezed again, his whole face contorting with desperation. Their guns roared simultaneously. But Rockwall's bullet must have jerked Laroque backward even as he fired, for his whole body tilted spasmodically, with the rifle jerking high, and Rockwall felt a whip of wind past his ear.

Laroque staggered backward a couple of steps, made an effort to halt himself, then spun around till he was turned the other way, and fell, full length, on his face in the brush. Rockwall rose to his full height, staggered to the man, turning him over. Laroque stared at him with the wide blank eyes of a man who had died instantly, with the bullet through his chest.

Rockwall turned and made his stumbling way as fast as he could down toward Tie. There was another shot before he reached the end of timber, and more granite chipped off in Tie's face.

"Toss me some dry beans for my wheel and I'll cover you while you make a run for it!" he shouted at Tie. Tie turned onto one side so he could thumb .44s from his gun belt, tossing them one at a time to Rockwall in the shelter of the timber. Rockwall jacked the wet shells from his Hopkins and Allen, shoving in the fresh ones.

"Any time, now," he said.

Tie took a last, strained glance up at the cliff, then jumped to his feet and ran headlong for the trees. Rockwall emptied his gun toward the cliff as he began running himself. It was too far for accuracy with a revolver, but the barrage must have spooked the bushwhacker, for there were no answering shots, and Tie threw himself safely behind a cottonwood. Rockwall followed him.

"Who was that down there?" panted Tie.

"Laroque," said Rockwall. "He's dead."

"Then that's Graves up on the cliff?" Tie asked.

"If it is, do you want to get him?"

"I'm tired of being bushwhacked."

"Then stay here and keep him interested," Rockwall murmured. "I'll try to work around that cliff and come on him from behind."

Their eyes met briefly. Rockwall turned to make his way heavily through the timber, passing Laroque's body with a glance. The reddened aspens quaked above him in a breeze. His passage crushed fallen grapes till his boots were blue with the juice. A wedge of Canada geese *honked* overhead. The silence, after they passed, was oppressive.

Rockwall traveled the timber banding the swift stream till he reached the end of that ridge, then turned across it to the next valley, from which the terrain of cliff and benches rose. This slope would bring him up on the opposite side of the cliff from which the bushwhacker had been shooting. The battering in the water and this forced run had drained him terribly, and it caused him painful effort to start the climb.

The slope was rocky and barren, with meager patches of buckbrush and drying monkey weed the only vegetation. Halfway up, the cliff became deeply fissured, and he sought one of these gullies for more cover. A little farther on, clumps of buckbrush choked it up again. He wormed through the first thicket of this, scratching face and hands. He was still within the brush when he had his first sight of the horse, hitched to some scrub juniper in a gully. It was not Graves's animal. It was a wild, hairy mare with a scarred apron face. The rigging puzzled Rockwall. It looked to be a Crow saddle, studded with brass tacks and hung with fringed, beaded saddlebags, and some of the tassels on the rawhide reins looked suspiciously like human hair. There was more brush choking the gully beyond. Rockwall rounded the horse and crawled into this next thicket. Almost to its upper edge, he saw that the gully petered out into a granite ledge. He was about to go on up when rocks began dribbling down the fissure.

Rockwall dropped down to where stunted hemlock choked the gully and forced his way into this for a screen. The man came sliding fast down through the talus. He wore an immense, shaggy buffalo coat, black and rotten with age, covering him to the thigh. His legs below this were clad in greasy leggings, long and skinny and loose-jointed as a drunk's. There was a sense of infinite age to his seamed face, yet his eyes had the bright, darting curiosity of a child's. He had a Mormon hat on, the brim pinned back to the crown with a bone needle, and his hair hung in long greasy tendrils like an aged squaw's, flapping in the wind.

"Whoa, 'Bakker!" he cried at the horse, as it began plunging and jerking at its hitch. "Here, 'Bakker!" And his voice held the deep, croaking gutturalization of a bullfrog. "There, 'Bakker, now, 'Bakker. . ."

"Hold it right there," Rockwall said. "I've got a gun on . . ."

Instead of dropping the immense old Sharps he held, the man wheeled toward Rockwall's voice, and the intent to shoot was plainly in his face. Rockwall wasn't going to be another target this day, and began firing at those skinny legs. His second shot knocked one from beneath the man.

"This third one will blow your head off," Rockwall told him, "if you don't get rid of that cannon."

Sprawled on the ground, the man spat gravel from his mouth, heaving the great Sharps away from him. "Damn' Injun," he said. "Damn' Flathead. Lyin' in the bushers that way."

Rockwall went up to him. "How long you been working for Graves?"

"Who'd work for that Kyesh?"

"We got Laroque down by the river," Rockwall told him.

The man rolled to an elbow, squinted up at Rockwall out of those bright eyes, began to chuckle. "Serves him right." He stopped laughing, and muttered peevishly: "Get me some 'bakker, damn you, my mouth's as dry as a summer crick."

" 'Bakker?"

" 'Bakker, 'bakker," snarled the old man, waving vaguely at the horse. "In them pouches some'ers. Don't you understand English?"

Rockwall had trouble getting near the hairy beast to search through the beaded saddlebags. He pulled out a handful of black powder and a half a dozen half-ounce balls mixed in with a string of beads and some rotting buckskin, finally coming up with a greasy, blackened plug of chewing tobacco. The pleased croak from the old man made him turn with it. The man bit off half of it and bulged his cheek out with it.

"Now some of that air Du Pont," he muttered, making juicy sounds with the tobacco. Rockwall dumped some of the loose gunpowder into his gnarled, serrated palm. The man turned to roll up the blood soaked leg of his rawhide britches. Then with a dirty bandanna off his neck he wiped the wound free, and spat a prodigious gob of yellow tobacco juice into the hole. Studying this a moment, he rubbed the black powder in after it, grinding the whole mess right into the wound with the heel of his hand.

"Heal in two days," he said. "Back on my feet and plugging at you afore you know it."

Rockwall squatted down, saying patiently: "Let's get all this straight, shall we? Who are you?"

"Handle of Kammas."

"Kammas what?"

"Kammas, Kammas, just Kammas!" exploded the old whang-hide. "Ain't that enough? I been Kammas for sixty years and I ain't added anything just to please a damn' Flathead dry-gulcher like your'n."

"All right," said Rockwall. "If you don't work for Graves, how come Laroque was in on this?"

"Graves sent Laroque out to me with a proposition of stopping you from getting Blue Boy. Sure, I says, why not, if you're damn' fool enough to give me help, I ain't refusing. Nobody's getting my Blue Boy, nobody's getting my doll."

"And if Graves had been trying to nail the roan, you'd have shot him up, too?"

"That's a fack, that's a true fack."

"You want Blue Boy for yourself."

"Nobody else," snarled the old man. "I been out here five years, five years, and, if I can't have him, nobody has him. Damn' horse runners, get my blue doll and sell him to a mutton-handed shorthorn like that Jennings . . ." Kammas was muttering to himself now, nodding his head from side to side and staring at the ground as if he had forgotten Rockwall's presence. "See 'ere what he did to that big red horse, Jennings and his mutton hands, ruined 'er, that's what he did. If that's the way they ride in Texas, I'll take bear grass. Nobody's going to get my Blue Boy and ruint him like that. Nobody but me has that roan, I tells 'em."

"Maybe I wouldn't turn Blue Boy over to Jennings if I caught him," murmured Rockwall.

Kammas's head lifted in a startled way. Then, slowly, his eyelids drew together in a suspicious squint. He turned to spit.

"I don't believe that. Graves thinks he can get five thousand from Jennings if he holds out. That kind of money blinds a man. You won't get Blue Boy. I'll see to it."

"You won't see it from here," Rockwall told him. "You're coming with me."

Tie came up. "Who's this old scarecrow?

"Calls himself Kammas."

Tie saw that the man was wounded. "Let's leave him here and get on after the roan."

"The roan?"

"Yeah," Tie said casually. "Neither of our horses was shot. We can pick them up. We know how the roan flushes now."

"Don't be crazy, Tie. We'll need a whole string of animals to ride him down. We'd kill our animals in a day, trying to keep up with him."

"He's tired now. We could find a box cañon."

"You know it's got to be planned better than that," Rockwall said. "What's got into you?"

Tie shook his head sullenly. "Nothing. I just don't see any point in waiting around."

Rockwall studied the boy narrowly. Was this the beginning of the breakup? He had seen what happened to other men when they lost their self-respect. Was Tie beginning to realize fully how much self-respect he had sacrificed in allowing Jennings to use him, in swallowing his pride and accepting Aldis with the tacit understanding that Jennings was really only trading her for the roan? Rockwall shook his head, hoping he was wrong. Perhaps it was just a boy's immaturity, with the pressure on. Tie had the sand to come through this.

"Let's swing this fellow on his horse and take him back with us," Rockwall said. "There'll be another day to catch that roan."

Kammas started cursing, but quieted suddenly, realizing that he was no match for the two of them.

"I'm also going to find Laroque's horse and sling him on," Rockwall said. "I want Graves to see exactly what happened. It might slow him down a little."

"Want me along?"

Rockwall shook his head. "You're too touchy. That's still Graves's town. We'd be pushing our luck too far by starting another ruckus."

"You taking this Kammas along, too?" Tie asked.

"No. Take him back to the ranch. We'll hold onto him. He's wounded so bad he won't give you any trouble. When I get back, maybe we can get something more out of him. See if you can get anything out of him in the meantime."

Rockwall watched him turn and go back after his horse. This was the way Rockwall wanted it. But he could not help remembering the time nothing had stopped Tie from joining him in town to buck Kenny Graves.

Chapter Eight

They got back to the ranch late that night, after Aldis had retired. Tie had some trouble getting Kammas into the house and putting him in Rockwall's room across the hall from the room he shared with Aldis. The wound in the old horse runner's leg was not infected, but it did render him incapable of escape. Tie thought it safe to leave him unguarded overnight.

Rockwall rode the night out, pushing himself and his horse to the utmost, reaching Hellgate about eight the next morning. The few men on the street stiffened in startled attention as he passed them, leading the other horse with Laroque's dead body slung across its saddle, head down. He hitched the animals before the Sapphire and went in.

A swamper was at work spreading sawdust on the floor; a single bartender was polishing and stacking glasses. Stanak was hunched over the far end of the bar, an eye opener halfway to his lips. He put it down as he saw Rockwall.

"One of you call Graves," Rockwall said.

"No need," Graves told him, stepping from behind the hanging that half hid the hall door. He was dressed in a flowered dressing gown with satin lapels and was wiping lather from his unshaven jaw with a big towel. "What's on your mind?" he said.

"Laroque is outside," Rockwall said. "I want you to see him."

Graves sent a puzzled glance to Stanak. Then he wiped the rest of the lather off his face, flung the towel at the bar, and came down the long room. The early risers had gathered in little knots around the dead man. Graves stopped at the curb, anger bringing a dull glow to his face beneath the blue-black stubble of his beard.

"I guess you know what happened," Rockwall said. "I'm tired of being jumped every time I run a bunch of wild ones out there. Now, if you want to keep this up, I'll wait here till the sheriff comes, and I'll tell everything I know at the inquest.

Everybody knows Laroque is your man. It'll make a big stink for you in this country. On the other hand, if you want to give up bushwhacking and tell me about the second man, I'll keep my mouth shut."

"The second . . . ?" began Graves, and then checked himself.

"Sure," said Rockwall. "Kammas, that old-timer with the Flathead mare."

Faint surprise showed in Graves's widening eyes. "Kammas?"

Rockwall realized they had both said too much. "You're saying he's not your man?"

Graves's eyelids, puffy with sleep, squinted almost shut. "I'm not saying anything, Rockwall."

Rockwall met his veiled gaze a moment. Then he went out to unhitch his horse and step aboard. He wheeled the animal around till he was facing Graves on the curb.

"Don't make the mistake of sending anybody else after us," he said.

"Maybe next time I'll come myself," Graves said.

Rockwall regarded him without speaking for a moment. Then he bent toward the man in a confiding way. "I hope you do, Graves," he said. "I just hope you do."

He reined the horse around and lifted it to a trot down the center of the street. He hit the Higgins Avenue bridge, and the sound of his horse's hoofs striking the planks filled the gorge below with a hollow boom. Then he was on the road winding up into the cañon.

He was thinking that he had learned more than he had bargained for, coming down here. So the old-timer who had attacked them in Hellgate Strip wasn't one of Graves's men. Kammas had been telling the truth. Graves had been surprised to hear that Kammas had been in the fight. He had been unable to hide that. But there had been more than surprise in the man's eyes before he had veiled what he felt. There had been anger, and a sharp calculation. Anger at what? The old-timer's interference? And calculation about what?

Rockwall frowned. If Graves would try this hard to stop him and Tie from getting the roan, it was logical he'd try just as hard to stop anybody else. Including Kammas? Rockwall had the feeling that something else was involved. He was convinced that he could find out from Kammas.

He pulled up on a height to see if he had been followed from town. Only one rider was leaving Hellgate, and he had turned south, along the road that would lead him into the Strip. Rockwall watched him a long time before he realized what this could mean. It was a strong possibility that Graves had sent a man out to get Kammas. Graves didn't know they had the old horse runner a prisoner.

Rockwall knew he had to reach Kammas right

off if he was to learn the full implications of what was happening. But his horse was too beat. He needed a new mount. The nearest spread was the Forked Tongue. He knew he was close to the breaking point now himself, but he couldn't let this pass. He turned the horse down the road and forced it into a trot.

It was early afternoon before he came into sight of that house set like a brandished fist up on the knoll. His horse was stumbling beneath him and he was reeling with exhaustion. He was still a quarter mile from the Forked Tongue outbuildings when he rounded a sharp turn and almost ran into Aldis on her Appaloosa. They both pulled up sharply, staring at each other in surprise. Then she reined in closer, and he saw that mature compassion darken her eyes.

"What is it? You've been riding all night?"

"Listen," he said, "there isn't time for questions. Can I switch horses with you?"

She studied his face a moment, lips parted with her hesitation. She wore one of her light silk shirts and denim riding breeches; her hair had been braided into two long plaits that fell across her shoulders. There was a shining, scrubbed look to her that robbed her of that sophisticated sheen, made her look like a little girl, shy and breathless. This reached him despite his exhaustion.

She swung down from her animal. "There's been trouble. Kammas got away during the night."

He dismounted with weary effort. Frustration had made him bitter. "Where's Tie?"

"Back at the ranch, waiting for you. He wants to go out after the roan."

"And you?"

"I came to Forked Tongue to see Uncle Black Jack."

"Do you know anything about Kammas?"

A frown curled her silken brows. "An old squaw man out in the Strip. Sort of a mystery. Nobody knows much about him."

"He's not Graves's man, though?"

"Heavens, no."

"If Graves found out Kammas was after Blue Boy, would he try to get the old man out of the way?"

"I imagine he would."

"Perhaps Kammas and I could join forces," Rockwall said.

She was peering into his face. "I don't imagine Graves would want that to happen. You're dangerous enough alone."

"I think that's what's happening," he said. "I've got to get to Kammas before Graves does."

Her lips parted, glistening like satin, and a sudden fear in her face brought her swaying toward him. "Rockwall," she breathed, "don't go alone, please."

He pulled back stiffly. "Aren't you forgetting something?"

She settled back, flushing. "I'm sorry," she said in a low voice. "It's just that I'm afraid for you."

The sincerity in her voice stirred him deeply. He touched her arm, starting to say something. The soft, satiny feel of it seemed to burn his palm, and he pulled his hand away self-consciously.

"I'll be all right," he said, digging his chin down, and then turned quickly to mount the Appaloosa, not wanting to see what was in her eyes any more. "Where'll you be?"

"Back at the ranch with Tie. First I'll change horses at Forked Tongue."

"I'll return your horse as soon as I can. I'm going to try to backtrack Kammas from where he tried to ambush us."

"Hadn't you better get Tie?"

"Why? He wasn't able to hold onto the old horse runner. I'll get him by myself."

He turned the animal off the road toward the hogback of the Garnets, heading in a straight line up over the ridge for Hellgate Strip on the other side. But he couldn't get the girl out of his mind. The eyes seemed to follow him, big and black and haunting.

It was late afternoon by the time Rockwall got back to the benchlands where they had been bushwhacked. It was not hard to pick up the old horse runner's trail. The tracks struck a game trail and followed it up a spur cañon onto the slopes of the Garnets. No attempt had been made to hide the trail. Probably the man had felt there was no reason to be cautious.

It was near sunset, and Rockwall was almost stupefied from exhaustion, when he topped a hogback and looked down into a shallow cañon where buckbrush grew raggedly and tamarack stood along the run-off course from a steep bank at the cañon's head. Beyond the scraggly line of timber stood a cabin of dovetailed pine poles and mud chinking, ancient and sway-backed, its thatched roof blackened from the smoke of an open-hearth fire whose outlet was no more than a vent. The scar-faced mare was grazing free, snuffling at dusty graze on this side of the tamarack. The wind was blowing toward Rock-wall, and the animal had not scented him. It was a lucky break that the old man had returned to his camp, but, then, where else would he go? Careful to keep out of sight, Rockwall hitched the Appaloosa and moved over the ridge in timber that kept him covered, then took a course down the slope that would not reveal him to the shack.

He watched for some sign of anyone else in the vicinity, but found none. That south fork out of Hellgate into the Strip would not get a man here any quicker than the route Rockwall had used. So if that man who had left Hellgate behind Rockwall was someone sent by Graves, Rockwall had a good chance of being the first here.

He gained the tamarack and poplars along the trickle of water. The timber was bunched in dense patches here, and beyond its tangled mat a sentinel peak had speared a falling ball of fire. Light spread in a crimson tide from this impaled sun as if it were flooding the world with its life's blood, to form ruddy pools of the open glades and cover the forest floor with a sanguine dappling. The foliage of the poplars caught it up thirstily, till each slick olive-green leaf gave off a brazen glitter. It made a tawny illusion of the shadows, to close about Rockwall like a dark mist whenever he left the patches of light.

At last Rockwall came again within sight of the cabin. The wild old man he had last seen up near the benchlands was sitting, leaning against the front wall. His chin was sunk deeply into his ragged buffalo coat, hair down over his eyes like frayed and greasy hemp. It looked as if he had fallen asleep on guard, for there was the old Sharps buffalo rifle across his lap.

Tension put an edge on Rockwall's nerves and dissipated his fatigue. But he did not move yet. The shadows lengthened and lost their warmth. Still the old man did not move. Rockwall was about to break toward him when a shrill whinny sounded from beyond the cabin. He froze.

But the old man did not seem to be roused. His head remained sunk heavily against his chest; he did not move. The whinny could have come only from the scar-faced mare. She couldn't have smelled Rockwall. The wind was still quartering against him. It meant someone was coming from beyond her.

Rockwall eased his Hopkins from its holster. If it was Graves's man, he would have to come around on this side to find Kammas.

The sun was gone completely now. The shadows had lost their tawny substance. They were swallowing up the timber about Rockwall with their hungry mouths. He had left his denim ducking jacket on the horse, and the chill began to eat at him. A hollow hooting broke against the stillness. His eyes ran along the hogback till they saw that it was only a grouse, squatting in the last patch of sun on the ridge. It sat with tail and wings hanging, filling its neck pouches with air till they looked swollen. Then the bird began pumping its head, deflating the pouches with those whistling hoots.

Slowly that last patch of sun abandoned the rocky ledge. When it was gone, the grouse gave a final *hoot*, and flapped away. Still Kammas had not moved from where he sat against the wall. His stillness was beginning to draw at Rockwall's nerves. His eyes ached from trying to penetrate the shadows. Then he thought he saw a flutter of motion to the right of the cabin. There was a faint glitter. The movement of a knife might make it.

This realization must have gone through him

the instant after he saw the glitter, for his gun was crashing in his hand. The knife made a deadly flicker from the trees. But it did not reach the house. It buried itself in the earth halfway between the trees and Kammas. And an instant afterward, Stanak was lurching from the undergrowth with a crash of brush, doubled over, his arms hugged across his belly. He took a couple of weaving, plunging steps, and then fell on his face. Only then did Rockwall realize he was standing, staring at the man.

"Drop your cutter before you turn this way," the old man said.

Rockwall knew a moment of frustrated anger. Then he dropped the Hopkins and continued to look at Kammas, still seated, leaning against the house, with the Sharps pointed at him.

"Go see if he's dead," Kammas said.

Rockwall moved stiffly over to Graves's man and rolled him over. The slackness of death took the sharp edges from Stanak's face, leaving it sallow and ugly.

"That was a good snap shot," said Kammas. "I never thought you'd make it." Rockwall stared incredulously and the old man cackled shrilly. "You young studs think you're so smart. I had you both pegged the minute you reached the valley."

Rockwall frowned at him, still unable to believe it. "Wasn't that taking a big chance?"

"Hell!" Kammas spat. "I've outjumped knives

before. Trick is to move just before they're throwed. I was ready to move when you shot. Why in thunder did you bother? Yesterday you tried to kill me."

"I thought you were with Graves yesterday," Rockwall said. "And I didn't try to kill you, anyway. You made me shoot."

Stringy jowl muscles began to move in Kammas's seamed face. His cheek was distended by a great cud of chewing tobacco. Rockwall noted that one leg of his buckskin breeches was badly stained with dried blood and had been slashed up one side, exposing a gnarled leg with skin like old leather. The bullet hole was through the fleshy part of the calf. It was a wonder the old man could have traveled so far as this with that wound.

"So you saved my life today," growled Kammas. "At least you tried to, whether I needed it or not. And now you think I ought to be grateful."

Rockwall could not suppress a wry grin. This was no senile old fool. There was acerbic humor to the man.

"If you don't work for Graves, why were you with Laroque yesterday?" Rockwall asked.

Kammas spat tobacco juice into a gnarled palm, clapped the hand against his leg, and ground the juice into the bullet hole. He leaned with a grunt to dip the hand into a beaded saddle-bag beside him and fill it with black gunpowder, which he rammed into the wound after the tobacco. It was the same doctoring he had done the previous day. Maybe it was working.

"Old mountain-man treatment," he snapped. "Healed me up enough to get back here." He spat aside. "I was working for myself yesterday. Like I told you, Graves sent Laroque up here to stop you from getting Blue Boy. Laroque came to me for help. Probably knew I'd line up against anybody who come out here and tried to grab my Blue Boy."

"But the roan's not yours."

"I've spent five years of my life follering that blue roan," Kammas said shrilly. "I ain't got him yet and maybe I never will, but nobody else will, either."

Rockwall had taken advantage of this talk to move a pace toward the man. "And if you saw Graves was after the roan, you'd turn around and bushwhack him?" he said.

"Damn right! I'd kill Blue Boy myself before I'd see Graves get him."

Rockwall took another step toward him. "Has Graves ever tried to kill you before?"

Kammas frowned at him. "I guess not."

"Then why should he send a man to get you now?"

"Dammee, I don't know."

"I'll tell you." Rockwall took another step. "It was because Graves was never afraid you'd catch Blue Boy alone. You might hang around the fringes of the herd and take pot shots at Graves when he tried to run the horse, but Graves could always chase you off. And you never got near enough to catching Blue Boy yourself to constitute any danger."

"That's a lie." Kammas waved an arm wildly. "I've been close enough to spit on that blue roan so many times. . . ."

"Have you?"

Kammas tried to meet his eyes. Then he emitted an uncomfortable growl and turned aside to spit.

"I thought so," Rockwall said. He was another pace nearer, and it would take only one more. "So Graves never thought you constituted any danger before. Why should he start worrying now? Because he was afraid I'd be looking for you. He was afraid, if you and I ever put our heads together, we might stand a chance of getting the horse."

Kammas's seamed hatchet face lifted sharply, eyes widening. The surprise in them gave Rockwall his chance. He took the last step in a jump, right leg kicking upward. Kammas shouted and moved the Sharps with a grunt. But Rockwall's boot lifted the barrel high, and the gun went off at the sky.

He came in behind the kick, wrenching the rifle from the old man's hands and tossing it aside.

Kammas lunged up from the wall and came into Rockwall, clawing and kicking. His strength surprised Rockwall, carrying him back and off balance for a moment. He grunted as one of those bony fists sank in his stomach. He tripped and knew he was falling, and grabbed the hoary edges of Kammas's buffalo coat, pulling Kammas with him.

He doubled his knees up as he hit, with his feet planted in the old man's belly. He rolled backward, jackknifing his legs out to throw Kammas over his head. He let himself go on into a backward somersault and came up on his feet, wheeling toward Kammas.

The man was just scrambling to his feet. Rockwall reached him before he was halfway up and hit him at the base of his neck. Kammas wheezed hard and went to his knees. He had just enough of his senses left to keep from sprawling flat. Rockwall went over and picked up his Hopkins. When he turned around, the old man was shaking his head dazedly.

"That wouldn't have happened if I hadn't let you get so close to me," he grumbled.

"And you wouldn't have let me get so close if you hadn't been so interested in what I was saying." Rockwall grinned. "And why were you so interested? Because it was true?"

"All right." The old man's eyes rolled in roguish discomfort. "So it was true. Mebbe Graves was

116

afraid for you and me to get together. I guess he knows how good you are at horse running, too. I admit I saw the way you ran them nags yesterday. You showed horse savvy the likes of which I ain't seen in a long time. You only ran them to see which way that roan flushed at the spooks, didn't you?"

"That's right. And he jumped just opposite from the way I figured he'd turn, every time."

"I never seen anybody besides me that ever figured that out," Kammas said. "Most of them just run him blind, don't notice how he acts at the spooks, just try to drive him into a box cañon or wear him down with relays, same's you'd catch any ordinary horse. They don't realize he ain't no ordinary . . ."

He caught himself, staring up at Rockwall in anger at having been drawn out so far. Rockwall grinned at him again.

"Maybe Graves was nearer the truth than he knew. Maybe you and me could catch that roan, Kammas. Why don't we try?"

"I ain't letting that roan fall into the hands of any saddle bum who'd sell him out the first offer that came along."

"What if I told you I wouldn't sell him out?"

"I wouldn't believe you," Kammas said.

Rockwall shrugged. "You're coming with me, anyway. I'm not leaving you out here to bushwhack me the next time I run the roan."

"You won't budge me."

"I will one way or the other. How'll you have it, easy or rough?"

Kammas squinted up at Rockwall, then shook his head disgustedly. "I guess I'm getting old. I'll have it easy."

Chapter Nine

They got back to the ranch late that night. Rockwall put the old man in his room, only this time he would be there to guard him, sleeping on the floor. The exertion of the ride had opened the wound again, and Kammas again applied his remedy. Tie was sleeping when Rockwell opened the door to the room he shared with Aldis. She wasn't there. The boy's head lifted from his bunk as Rockwall entered.

"Got Kammas back," Rockwall told him. "I brought him along. This time he'll stay put. I think he can help us with Blue Boy, and it'll be easier to have him with us than against us. I saw Aldis down near the Forked Tongue. Borrowed her Appaloosa. Where is she?"

"She went to the Forked Tongue, all right," Tie said disconsolately. "She and Black Jack had a fight and they both had necks full of hell. When she got back here, she was so jumpy, she started spatting with me, and I left and headed for town. I took the short cut in. Aldis told me she'd run into you and that you were off backtracking that old fossil. I figured you'd get him, but I couldn't see the point. We pulled his fangs. He's too stove up to make any more trouble. It was late in the afternoon when I hit town."

"Get in any trouble?"

"Just the opposite. Graves tried to proposition me. He seemed to think you wouldn't be able to get Blue Boy without me. He offered me a soft spot with him if I'd break with you."

Rockwall stared at Tie, puzzled by the strange half smile on the boy's lips. "And?"

Tie dismissed it with a casual gesture. "I told him I wanted the horse as bad as you. Then he gave me a different offer. He made it plain that, if we got the horse, he'd do everything in his power to keep us from realizing anything on it. He told me he'd lay off, though, if I agreed to hand the horse over to him when it was broke, and he'd go halves with me on what Jennings gave for it."

Rockwall stared at the floor. "I get the impression Graves doesn't care much about the roan or the money he'll get out of it. Do you think Graves would have made this kind of offer to you if he'd known you were married to Aldis?"

"I don't think so. I sure didn't tell him about it."

"Maybe he doesn't know," Rockwall said. "Or maybe he was just sucking you in." He shook his head, too played out to follow it further. "Where's Aldis?"

"Don't know. She was gone when I got back. No note, nothing. I knew she wasn't with Graves. Figured maybe she went back to the Forked Tongue for another go-around with Black Jack."

Rockwall thought Tie should probably keep better track of his wife, but, knowing Aldis, he also figured that was probably impossible. She had seemed so anxious to get away from Black Jack, and, if Tie was right, she had been to see him twice in one day.

"We're hitting the Strip again tomorrow," Rockwall said. "We've had the devil's own luck catching any wild ones at all with only one saddle animal apiece. That blue roan's going to take a lot of running. We'll need a whole string of animals to switch off on before we even start thinking about going after him."

"How about Jennings's remuda?" Tie wondered.

Rockwall shook his head. "His saddle strings are out on roundup. Those we could get at the home ranch aren't worth putting a saddle on. You know how he treats his animals."

"Yeah. Aldis had a plug when she came back." Grumbling, Tie then rolled over with his face to the wall.

Rockwall went to his room, laid blankets on the floor, saw the old man was slumbering, and almost instantly fell asleep himself.

He awoke late the next morning to find Kammas hobbling painfully around in the kitchen, getting breakfast. When Rockwall and Tie left, they took with them the old man's mare and the horses they had brought in from the Strip the last time. Rockwall did not think Kammas would try to escape again without an animal, especially with his leg in that condition.

It took them a couple of days to scout out a likely section, set up a fresh trap, and flush a bunch into it. From the dozen wild, plunging animals in the pen, they culled out seven, leaving five possibilities. These they hobbled and headed back to the ranch. According to Kammas, who was alone at the ranch, Aldis had been in and out. At first Tie had wanted to try and find her, but changed his mind. She got back later that night. By that time Rockwall was asleep, although the old man was still up, in the kitchen.

The next morning Rockwall got down to the corral early. Soon Tie joined him and they started again to work. One at a time they turned the wild mustangs into the pen, tying tow sacks of earth on their backs and letting them buck themselves out. They did the same thing with a saddle next. By the time Tie stepped on, a lot of vinegar had been taken out of the broncos, saving him a beating.

The first one Tie broke was a little chestnut. As soon as Rockwall took him over to gentle, he saw he was prime material. The horse had the painful refinement and the deep suspicion of an animal born wild, and had probably been sired in one of the bands on the Strip. The second one Tie broke was a buckskin mare. Once broken to the saddle, she showed a casual ease with men, which indicated she might have originally run with some outfit's saddle stock, escaping to join the wild bunch before she could be branded. This buckskin went 200 or 300 pounds heavier than the chestnut. She did not possess her talent, but her size and bottom would make a good animal for the severe winters up here.

Working this hard, Rockwall saw little of Aldis. He had noted a sullen tension once in a while between Tie and the girl, but he marked that off to the inevitable spats of the newly married. The old horse runner was hobbling around on a cane now, the wound in his leg actually healing. He had come down to watch them working the horses when Rockwall had to bring the buckskin back to Tie. Aldis had come along with Kammas.

She brushed jet hair away from one cheek, smiling at Rockwall. "Tie tells me the two of you aren't getting along too well." She paused. The silence seemed awkward. Kammas cleared his throat and spat. "You go ahead and work," she said. "Tie told me how anxious you were to get a good saddle string before winter hits. We'll just watch."

Rockwall nodded. "Maybe you'd better take another ride on that buckskin, then, Tie. You didn't get all the vinegar out yesterday."

"She wasn't bucking when I finished," Tie growled.

"She is now." Rockwall stared closer at the boy. "What's eating you?"

"Nothing."

"Then how about giving the buckskin another ride?"

"I rode her out, I tell you. A man gets tired twisting his guts up all day long on the green stuff."

"You knew what it would be like," Rockwall said. "Are you backing out?"

"I'm not saying I won't bust the stuff for you."

"Then what *are* you saying? All that's left is the polishing. Is that what you mean? What would you do with a buckskin that started fence-worming the minute you climbed on?"

"She broke straight when I was riding her."

"You were using the spurs then, too," Rockwall said. "You're not busting her now . . . remember? No spurs, no rough stuff."

Tie stepped aboard. He urged her into a trot with his heel. Then she broke into a twisting gallop, almost pitching Tie off.

"Whoa, you knot-headed broomtail!" he yelled, hauling up.

The buckskin reared with the pain of the knot under her jaw. Anger twisted Tie's face as he dug spurs into the horse. She squealed and whirled into a zigzag run.

"Take those spurs out of her!" yelled Rockwall.

The buckskin veered, quartering toward him, and he ran in to her, grabbing the hackamore and pulling her down.

"Let go!" snapped Tie, trying to jerk the horse away with a violent pull on the reins. "I'll handle her."

"If you're polishing her, you're not going to use those spurs," Rockwall said. "Get down here and take them off."

"I don't take my spurs off for nobody."

"Then you'd better get off the horse."

"I will not."

"Either you get off, Tie, or I'll take you off."

The boy grew rigid in the saddle, staring down at Rockwall, anger twisting his face. Then, slowly and stiffly, he dismounted. He had his fists clenched, and for a moment Rockwall thought he meant to use them. Finally, however, the boy spun on a heel and stalked off toward the house. Aldis flung a strained look at Rockwall, then ran after Tie. She grabbed at his arm, saying something. He tore loose so hard she stumbled and almost fell. But she followed him on toward the house, speaking intensely. Kammas watched them go with a wry grin on his face.

"Jist had to show off in front of the gal."

Rockwall was watching them, too, a sick feeling at the pit of him. "I think it goes deeper than that, Kammas. Tie's been jumpy a long time."

"It still goes back to the gal," Kammas said. "He's too damn' rough for my money . . . with horses and women."

Rockwall turned to glance at him. Then he went and got the buckskin. It took him an hour of hard work to quiet the horse. Talking to her, gentling her, walking her around the corral, he finally had her obedient again.

"You really talk her language," Kammas told him, chuckling. "Tie has a lot to learn if he thinks he can pick up what you know about polishing in a few days. You're mighty young to know so much about horses, Rockwall."

"Some are born with it," Rockwall said. "I never was very good on the rough string. Just never liked to hurt them that much."

"Do you think that boy has it in him?"

"Tie? Maybe."

"If that woman would stop picking at him."

Rockwall looked up at him. "It *was* her, then."

"Sure," said the old man. "I couldn't help hearing them talk in the kitchen this morning. She put it in his mind, how you was taking it so easy and he was doing all the dirty work. How he ought to quit the rough stuff so he wouldn't be so tired and beat up all the time and he could take her to a little high life down in town. She's got big ideas, that girl. She sees you got a lot of horses here. She thinks you can train them in a couple of weeks and sell them all for big prices so she can spend it down in Hellgate on good times."

"Oh . . ." Rockwall shrugged it away. "I don't think it's that bad."

The old man spat his tobacco juice. "I ain't exaggeratin'. I thought she'd bitten his head off when he kicked about her getting in so late from her uncle's last night."

"Her uncle's?" Rockwall frowned. "I thought Jennings had gone to the rodeo in Billings?"

"So did I." The old man leered. "Aldis and Tie were really goin' 'round and 'round. Reg'lar Crow war dance."

"No wonder he was so touchy," murmured Rockwall. "I guess it was my fault. I shouldn't have jumped him that way."

"You're touchy yourself," said Kammas. "You both been working too hard. Anything's liable to set it off."

Rockwall looked up at the man, something else entered his mind, something formed from an idea that had been there ever since he had brought Kammas back with him. "When Aldis was gone, you were all alone here. All alone and able to walk on that leg."

Kammas cackled like an old squaw. "I suppose I could have got away, at that."

"Why didn't you?"

"Same reason you wanted to keep me here so long."

"I thought it would be easier to run the wild ones without you bushwhacking us every trip," Rockwall told him.

"That wasn't the only reason you brought me back here," said Kammas. "You thought I'd be around and see how good you was with the horses and maybe make some kind of deal about Blue Boy."

"Maybe I did," said Rockwall. "You've been on his tail five years, you say. You must know more about him than any other man."

"So I do. And so you *are* good with the horses. So good that when you talk to them, it's like you was talking another language. I don't even understand the words. Their language, mebbe. And so mebbe a man like me couldn't catch Blue Boy, or a man like you, but if we threw in together, like you suggested back at my camp, maybe the two of us could. That still don't mean you wouldn't sell him if you got him."

"You wouldn't even have stayed here this long if you really believed that," said Rockwall.

Kammas looked at the buckskin again, mingled emotions tugging his face from one expression to another. "You really love them, don't you?"

"It's like I told you. That's why I never made good on the rough string. I hated to put them through the punishment."

Kammas leaned forward, sober and intent as a child. "And you really wouldn't sell the roan to Jennings?"

"If he's as good as he looks, I won't sell him to anybody," said Rockwall. He saw the indecision tearing Kammas, and thought it was the time to press in. "If you caught him by yourself, how did you expect to break him anyway?" he asked.

Kammas stiffened proudly. "I'd break him."

"You know you couldn't, you old fool," said Rockwall affectionately. "When a man gets as old as you and me, his bones won't take a beating like that. I would have come apart riding out an ordinary horse, like this buckskin. Think what an animal like that roan would do to me. Or you."

Kammas seemed to shrink, turning his eyes to the ground. "What about Tie?"

"If anybody can bust Blue Boy, it's him. He'll do it."

Kammas bent toward him in a sudden confidence. "I'm an old man, Rockwall, older'n you think. This would be my last trick. I run horses when the cattle in this state was buffalo. I'd hate to count the wild ones I trapped. Most of my life has been spent with it. And in all that time I never saw one like Blue Boy."

Rockwall put his hand on Kammas's shoulder.

"You wouldn't be talking this way to me unless you had some faith in my word. How much faith do you have?"

"Just give it to me. Just say you'll keep him here and let me sit on him once in a while, let me ride him down to Hellgate and show them greenhorns what a real horse is."

"We'll keep him here," said Rockwall. "And you'll ride him whenever you want."

The old man's eyes shone wetly, and then he turned away in embarrassment, making a lot of noise in his expectoration. Rockwall saw his throat work a little. He cleared it, turning back, and his voice had a guttural, confiding tone. "Ever hear of the Echo Pit?"

Chapter Ten

They did not sight Blue Boy again till after the first snow. Tie and Rockwall were into Hellgate Strip then, after another wild bunch, and they came upon the roan and his band cropping at the sere grass along the bottoms of River Rock. He must have been hiding out in the badlands all this time, for the whole bunch of them looked gaunted. Rockwall did not flush them, but sent Tie back to get Kammas at the ranch, and then camped on Blue Boy's tail. When the bunch moved, he marked his trail with strips cut from his yellow slicker and tied to branches along the way, in case another snow covered his trail.

Tie and Kammas came up with him next morning, back in the Sapphires. They had a string of extras from the ones Rockwall had gentled, and food for a week. Kammas would not talk much till they had climbed to one of the higher crests, on the trail of the drifting band. From here, a vast panorama spread out on all sides. The foothills undulated away northeastward into the serrated badlands of Hellgate Strip and the damask Garnets beyond. To the south and north the ridges of the Sapphires spread like the hairy fingers of a hand, with the valleys swallowed by their own shadows between. Blue Boy was visible, dropping into one of these valleys now. Kammas halted his hairy 'Bakker, and Rockwall knew he was going to speak finally.

"We'll have to turn him back now," muttered the old man. "The Echo Pit is mebbe twenty miles south and fifteen or twenty east of here."

"I still think this is a lot of work for nothing," said Tie, huddling into his Mackinaw. "I've seen enough horses in a place that echoes. It don't bother them much."

"You never been in the Echo Pit," said Kammas. "You'll see what I mean when we get there. It drives the animals crazy. I've seen wild ones go so loco in there they keep running at a rock wall till they've butted themselves to death. I've tried a dozen times to run Blue Boy in there, but I couldn't do it alone. If we can do it this time, it'll drive him so crazy he'll lose all that cunning of his and we can turn him any way we want."

Tie made a disgruntled sound into the uplifted collar of his coat. Kammas ignored it, biting off a chew of tobacco.

"We're going to have to get ahead of him now," said Kammas, "and drive him by spooks. Tie, you stay here and keep pushing from behind. Don't crowd him. Just let him see you now and then. Got 'er?"

Tie nodded. Kammas glanced at Rockwall, then turned to spur 'Bakker away. Rockwall had the impulse to say something but, seeing the sullen line of Tie's shoulders, knew it would be useless. He picked the lead line of three spare animals from Tie's hand, and pushed after Kammas.

They drove hard to get ahead of Blue Boy, dropping down off the ridge on this side to be hidden, watching the shift of wind carefully. They reached a saddle and went through, sighting Blue Boy about half a mile behind them in the next valley. They dropped down through heavy snowdrifts into the lower timber, hunting for a spot to spook him. Finally they found it, where the creek turned sharply from its northward course and pointed due west for 100 yards.

On the south bank, after the turn, timber crowded right down to the water and the north was a cutbank twenty feet high, with deep, rocky stretches of water beneath. The horses could not climb this cutbank. This left them two alternatives —either the shallows of the south bank, or the timber. An ordinary horse would have chosen the shallows, but they knew Blue Boy too well now.

"Do you think Tie has the savvy to see this spot?" Kammas asked.

"He'll be riding high enough behind the roan to see this a mile away," said Rockwall. "He's been working with me long enough to know what kind of a spot I'd pick. Don't worry about him."

It was tricky enough to gauge which way a normal horse would turn when it met a spook. But to base your judgment on a horse that turned just the opposite from the expected, and use his very cunning to drive him, was a maddeningly delicate job.

Kammas took out a paper sack they had just emptied of coffee, sticking it on a bush at the turn of the creek. The man smell on this sack would turn an ordinary wild horse onto the northern bank. But Rockwall wanted Blue Boy to turn south, and was counting on his perversity. Then they went through the water past the high bank to where the creek again veered north. Here they splashed out of the shallows and rose to the slopes beyond, finally reaching a meadow from which they could watch what happened below.

Sure enough, Tie had guessed this would be the first spook, and had driven the horses into it. Blue Boy came trotting out of timber, head up, tail switching, a magnificent picture of horseflesh. He halted a moment, within sight of the spook, and they knew he was snorting, although they could not hear it. Then, instead of taking that logical, easy way down the shallows, he turned southward into the dense timber. The band had a hard time scrambling up that steep, sandy cutbank, and Blue Boy slid down half a dozen times to urge on a faltering animal. Finally they were all on dry land again.

Kammas grinned tightly. "That devil, just the opposite from any ordinary horse. Only now he's going the way we want." He poked guthooks to his mare.

They rode hard again to get ahead of Blue Boy, finding another spot in his path where they could use his own perversity to turn him farther southward, planting a spook that would have turned a normal horse to the north, but which he inevitably allowed to turn him in the other direction. When they finally had him turned down the valley, they pushed him due south for twenty miles. They had to crowd him to get through Shalkaho Pass.

It was nearly dusk when they reached Shalkaho Pass with the hooting cry of fool hens echoing down the ancient aisles of yellow pine. They had been traveling fast ahead of the horse to plant their spooks, but now they pulled up to wait and get one more glimpse of him before dark.

Their last spook was a strip of red cloth at the mouth of a broad gully. The alternative route away from this gully was through a long, sloping meadow littered with the toppled, charred logs of some ancient fire, and studded with blackened stumps. It formed a veritable maze for a horse to run, and any ordinary animal would have avoided it.

Blue Boy halted there longer than usual, head switching from side to side. A strange indecision filled his movements. But finally he turned off into the meadow, picking his way painfully, carefully through the blackened stumps and labyrinth of charred logs, nervous and whinnying. A frown knotted Rockwall's brow.

"I think he's going to start switching saddles," he said.

Kammas looked sharply at him. "What do you mean?"

"We've been driving him long enough with his own trick. I think he's beginning to sense it. He's going to start turning the tables on us and take the ordinary run away from a spook."

Kammas looked at him for a moment, a slow grin spreading over his gnarled face. "I think you might be right, and I think, if somebody was to come on you during a full moon, and catch you with your pants down, they might find a horse's tail sprouting out of your hindquarters."

Rockwall grinned wearily, shrugging. "It's just a feeling I have."

"We'll abide by it," said Kammas. "But it's going to be hell in the dark."

They tried to place the first one before dark, to see if Rockwall was right. Blue Boy was leading his band straight through the pass, and they cut around him till they came to a stream. The pass narrowed here and would funnel the running band right into a ford. The serviceberries and other brush were so thick along the near bank that it looked impenetrable, except for a hole ten feet broad worn through it by countless centuries of game travel.

They planted their spook here so that the alternatives were this hole or the heavy brush on either side. Then they crossed the ford and watched from timber beyond, where they could not be seen by the horses. If he kept turning from the spook the way he had been doing, Blue Boy would veer aside into the brush, avoiding the hole. The men sat tensely on hipshot horses. Rockwall's eyes began to ache with peering. Then abruptly the heavy-chested roan appeared in that hole which led to the ford, his band following.

"You were right," breathed Kammas. "He's

switched ends. You must be half horse, Rock-wall."

"It's going to be touch and go from now on," muttered Rockwall. "No telling what he'll do."

Tie came up with them, bringing fresh horses, and Kammas explained the strategy. Throughout the night, Blue Boy did not change back to his old trick. They allowed him to drift of his own accord, planting only one or two spooks. From these, he chose the avenue any normal horse would. At dawn, they let him water at Shalkaho Falls. Then they started veering him south once more, across the Bitterroot Valley into the mountains beyond.

All three men were so weary by now they began dozing in the saddle, keyed up with the grueling ride, the sleepless night, the tension of constantly having to outthink the cunning horse. The band of wild ones themselves were showing the strain, flushing like quail at the slightest disturbance, taking long, wild, unnecessary runs whenever the men were careless enough to let the horses catch sight of them.

Blue Boy began switching back and forth now. At one spook he would shy back into his old trick, taking the illogical avenue. At the next, he would pick the ordinary way.

"We're through with the arithmetic now," Kammas told Rockwall. "It's up to your horse sense. Can you outguess him all the way into the Bitterroots?"

The dust and sweat had formed a grimy mask over Rockwall's face, wrinkled and cracked about his eyes and mouth, streaked with new perspiration. He felt himself sagging in the saddle, an overpowering desire for sleep sweeping him momentarily. But there was a devilish, driving excitement to the chase, known only to the initiate, a strange exhilaration that could approach hysteria near the end of the run. It left the mind clear, lending it the abnormal sensory capacities of a high fever, or a trance, filling it with keen, biting, lucid perceptions that extended far beyond any normal limits.

"We'll get him," said Rockwall.

They changed to fresh horses. Rockwall was now on that buckskin, with her bottom, not as talented as the chestnut in the quick fast work, but a good animal for the grind. It was the hardest, wildest chase Rockwall had ever known. All day long he pitted all his knowledge, all his skill, all his remarkable understanding of horses against the wily cunning of that blue roan.

It was a battle now. No longer was the beast being driven. He was fighting at every spook. He became so unpredictable that the men lost him time after time, and, if it had not been for Tie, who was back there on his tail, the horse would have backtracked out of their reach. But the Texas boy could reach the same frenzy of excitement that gripped Rockwall in this stage of the chase, and he was priceless in his rear position. It began to snow that afternoon, easing their job a bit. The drifts in many sections soon piled up too deeply for the horses, limiting their avenue, and the men could drive them more easily.

Finally they had the band right up against a great granite escarpment that seemed to touch the sky. The snowfall had stopped, and the world lay in pristine alabaster silence all about them. The Echo Pit came into view, a narrow cut through the escarpment, with walls 100 feet high, building up into lithic mosques and minarets and cups and hollows that provided the weird acoustics.

"He's going to go loco now," said Rockwall. "It's no use trying to direct him with those spooks any more. All we can so is plant so many spooks it will confuse him completely, and then come in on his tail and his flanks and drive him right for that cañon."

"There's a trail up over the cliff," said Kammas. "I want to take it and reach the other end of the Echo Pit. Once inside, none of us would ever be able to pass the roan and block him when he hit the other opening. Give me time to get around there, half hour, mebbe. Then push like hell."

Rockwall nodded, watching the old man get off the animal he had been riding and go over to 'Bakker, refreshed by a few hours' traveling without a rider. On the hairy mare, Kammas started for the trail winding its way up through the granite outcroppings and disappearing at last in the hemlock and juniper on top of the plateau.

Rockwall waited here till Tie came up. The boy's long body sagged in the saddle, hands listlessly against the saddle horn. But there was a feverish light in his eyes that came from more than exhaustion, and he straightened up when Rockwall told him this was it. Now all the tension between them was gone, and the rapport of the old days gripped them. They each picked a fresh horse, picketing the others in timber, and they were ready.

In his position behind the band, Tie had picked up many of the spooks Kammas and Rockwall had planted as he passed them. Now he gave these to Rockwall, and Rockwall planted them again, all about the approach of the giant crevice. Then he returned to Tie, figuring Kammas had reached the other end by then, and they began to maneuver the band in on the spooks.

They were crowding them when the roan came upon the first one. No hesitation now. He shied wildly to the right into a ravine. Rockwall had put spooks at the end of this, and the horse appeared suddenly on the lip, veering away from them and out of the ravine again. Back and forth, circling, cutting back on himself, the horse ran, leading his band and the two riders a wild chase.

The buckskin was flagging beneath Rockwall, and Tie's horse was stumbling. Finally they got the band to running through a thick stretch of willows that thinned out near the opening of the Echo Pit. With the long brown shoots clattering at his legs, Rockwall caught sight of Tie on the opposite flank of the herd, and shouted hoarsely at him.

"If he goes as far as the mouth, try like hell to drive him away from it! Don't let him in that mouth if it kills you!"

He saw the surprise lift in Tie's chin, then the understanding in the stiffening of his body. They burst from the willows into the alkali flats spreading out from the sandy bottom of the gorge. Tie was on the inside of the bunch, and it fell to him to work Rockwall's ruse. He had to draw blood from his horse before it would go into another headlong run that brought it up even with the animals. Blue Boy's first reaction, when he caught sight of the Texas boy, was to veer away. Rockwall dropped back to let him through if he wanted. The roan saw the opening and started to take it. Then he must have realized how hard Tie was driving him away from the mouth of that gorge, and in a sudden fit of his old perversity, wheeled and made a feint at it.

Tie spun his horse and raced back the other way to block the roan. Blue Boy shifted from his feint and headed at a headlong gallop for the gorge. Then, in that last instant, when he was past Tie, he seemed to slow down and start an indecisive, veering motion, as if suspecting he had been trapped.

Rockwall spun the bay on his heel and put his spurs in his guts, racing the laboring, heaving animal across the alkali in a screaming, shouting attempt to get ahead of Blue Boy and turn him back from the gorge. It must have looked genuine enough to convince the roan. His indecision stopped and he plunged headlong into the great chasm. With a wild, crazy grin of admiration at Rockwall, Tie drove his animal in after the roan, not even waiting for the rest of the band. They broke in a dozen different directions away from the gorge.

Then Rockwall was deep in the shadows of the great, yawning pit. It wound back and forth like a snake in spasms of agony. Gigantic cracks in the walls of the main gorge had been caused by some ancient shift of the crust here, and these formed spur cañons every few feet, some not wide enough to get an arm into, others twenty or thirty feet broad. And the echoes began.

There were stretches of ice on the bottom that crackled like ripping cloth beneath the horse's drumming hoofs. This sound rippled down the cañon till Rockwall thought it had been swallowed. Then, suddenly, Rockwall found himself staring up, thinking that the walls were cracking apart. He realized it was the echoes of those hoofs on ice, coming back now, multiplied, magnified a hundredfold, forming a wild, maddening cacophony that filled the narrow gorge, rising and falling, bouncing back and forth from one wall to the other. Then they were off the ice and clattering across a rocky shelf. The sound of hoofs was puny compared with the echo it brought.

It seemed as if the whole world was roaring and rocking about him, and he thought his head would burst with it. Rockwall's horse started squealing and whinnying and fighting the hackamore. They could see Blue Boy ahead of them, rearing up, wheeling from one wall to the other, eyes white, chest lathered.

Then the roan saw them coming in from behind, and turned to race away again. There was no calculation to his escape now, however. It was a headlong dash, ears flattened, mane flailing the air like a dusty pennant.

Rockwall did not think there could be louder sound. But it came. Like the screaming of a banshee it came. Gargantuan shouts. Gigantic yells. Immeasurable vocables rolling down the gorge toward them and undulating them in the waves of a measureless ocean of noise.

Kammas came into view, his mouth open in the shouts, beating his leggings with that old horse thief hat. Rockwall took the cue and started yelling himself. He could not hear his voice, but the echoes came back to him in burgeoning waves, mingling with all the multiplied madness of the other echoes that never seemed to die.

Under ordinary circumstances, Blue Boy might not have wheeled away from Kammas. But he was already showing the effect of this awesome, frightening place. He turned away from the oncoming man, back toward Tie and Rockwall. Seeing them, he whirled again. His eye caught one of those spur cañons, and he started towards it. Then he halted, as if sensing a trap. Rockwall pulled out his gun and began to shoot.

The echoes of the shots filled the gorge with such incalculable sound that the walls actually seemed to tremble with it, reeling inward. With this terrible new shock of sound crashing against him, the blue beast lost the last of his poise, rearing up in an agony of maddened frenzy. All his cunning obliterated by that primal fear of this vast noise, all his uncanny knowledge of man, his calculated timing, his almost human understanding failed him, and he broke, froth dripping from his muzzle, to plunge headlong into that spur cañon.

Within 100 yards, the fissure narrowed down till a horse could no longer pass through, and at that point the roan had to stop, marbled with lather down to the knees, blood flecking the foam dripping from his snout, eyes like white china in his head.

Rockwall flicked his rope out, dabbing the loop over the roan's head. The animal charged the three men, running right into Rockwall's noose. The shock knocked Rockwall's horse against Tie. But Tie put down a mangana that caught the roan's forehoofs, and Blue Boy fell heavily against Rockwall's horse and slid on down to the ground, unable to keep upright with its forefeet scissored by the rope.

Rockwall stepped off the buckskin and threw the slack of his own clothesline about the roan's hind hoofs, hog-tying the horse. Then Kammas and Tie dismounted, and they all three stood staring at the great, heaving, writhing blue beast.

"Y'know," breathed Kammas at last, "I'm almost sorry we did it."

Chapter Eleven

It took them three days to get Blue Boy back, hobbled so that he could travel at nothing greater than a slow trot, a man on either side with a rope on his neck. Even then he fought them every step of the way. Once back, they all needed a rest. Rockwall slept the clock around. Tie and Kammas, who now slept in the tack room in the barn, were still rolled in their blankets after Rockwall was out catching up with the chores. They did not try to work the roan that day or the next. Blue Boy needed a rest as much as they, after the terrible chase.

It was a Wednesday that they cleaned a corral of snow and brought the roan out for his first test, hobbled by Rockwall and Kammas. The horse now had a couple of days' rest and good feeding behind him, and was in good enough shape to judge his true worth. There was a sense of potent, almost sinister power in his low-slung frame. Running wild, he had not put on all the weight he could, and, although he probably touched 1,000 pounds now, he could carry 1,200 easily. His neck was heavy by some standards, but it had a classic arch, and the immense throttle held the wind of an Arab. The dominant blood was probably Quarter, with that heavy rump, so prodigiously muscled it looked almost grotesque from some angles. But the refinement of his bones and the high set of his tail and that big throttle pointed to a lot of Morgan or Arab somewhere.

Beginning to liven up, he wheeled back and forth around the corral, snorting and pawing, dragging Kammas and Rockwall with him, and with every turn the rump muscles came into play, rippling and bunching with the immense power that gave the Quarter animals such explosive speed in the jump-off so dear to a cowman's heart.

"All right," Tie growled. "Are we just going to stand and look, or are we going to start putting the devil to some good use?"

Rockwall sensed Kammas's quick anger. Blue Boy meant only one thing to Tie; he could never understand how Rockwall and the old horse runner felt about this roan. It would do no good to explain. A showdown would have to come, but this wasn't the time for it.

They spent that first week trying to teach him to understand the rope, hours a day in the corral throwing it on his neck and taking a dally around the snubbing post in the center to bring him up short. But he never ceased to fight it. Finally they put the tow sack on. He boiled over and kept hitting the clouds for half an hour straight, going higher than Rockwall had ever dreamed a horse could jump. When it became evident that he would continue bucking and never stop until he had ruined himself, Rockwall took his life in his hands and ran in to tear off the sack.

It was this way for another week, while the days ran together, and in his grim absorption Rockwall lost count of time. They finally gave up and strapped on the saddle. This was no more successful. The horse bucked till blood was running from his nostrils and his body was covered with dirty yellow foam, and again Rockwall had to go in and stop him for fear he would buck himself to death.

They all knew it was not uncommon for horses to do this, and yet break under a man, but the savagery Blue Boy displayed kept Rockwall or Kammas from saying anything. Tie brought it up, after they had fought the beast for two weeks, and Rockwall felt a deep pride in the boy for it. They were at breakfast Saturday morning when Tie put down his fork and looked at the wall.

"There isn't any use going out there and putting an empty kak on him again today. If he was going to get used to the tree, he'd be quiet under it by now. How about letting me step on?"

Aldis whirled from the stove, where she had been getting coffee. "Oh, Tie, if you do it today, you'll be too beaten to take me down to Hellgate this evening. I'm sick and tired of sitting up here, staring at the four walls while you play with that stupid animal. It's been two weeks now and we haven't been off the place. Eighteen hours a day, coming in too tired to say good night to me, getting up too early to eat breakfast with me. . . ."

She trailed off at the utter silence that met this. Both Kammas and Rockwall were still looking at Tie, for they had sweated on the roan all this time with the boy, and knew the implications of what had just been said. But neither of them put it into words.

"This is Saturday," said Rockwall. "We can lay off a couple of days and see how he is on Monday."

Tie shook his head. "The lay off would only put more vinegar in him. Maybe you'd be happy to watch him buck that damned saddle till next Christmas. I wouldn't. My job here is to ride the jumps out of him. I'm tired of waiting."

Aldis said: "Tie, if you do this, I won't be here to make your supper tonight. I'm going down to Uncle Black Jack's, I swear."

Tie got up from the table so violently he upset his chair. It made a heavy clatter in the silence. He looked at Aldis with his mouth open, as if to say something in anger. Then, without speaking, he wheeled and stalked out the door.

With a heavy sigh, Rockwall got up. "Take it easy on the kid, will you, Aldis?" he said without much enthusiasm.

Her eyes flashed at him, and she turned away with a sullen pout to her lower lip.

Kammas was staring at Rockwall reproachfully, and Rockwall felt sudden irritation at the way the conflicting ambitions of these three were squeezing him. He followed Tie out, anger growing in him at the way everyone who wanted this horse saw in it the means of fulfilling some personal desire.

A tight chute between a small holding pen and a big working corral was standard equipment with most horse outfits, but they had never been forced to use theirs before. It took the three of them half an hour to get Blue Boy in the chute. They put a war bridle on his snout and a Scotch hobble that pulled his left hind leg off the ground, and he still fought them with grim, unrelenting vigor. When they finally got him in the squeezer,

148

Kammas got six inches of flesh taken off the side of his face reaching through to throw off that hobble.

Blue Boy tried to batter the chute apart, but it was too tight for much violent movement, and the cramped position finally subdued him into a sullen, deceptive quiescence. There was an awesome, frightening threat to his small, ugly shifts back and forth, a bestial portent to the animal heat of him, emanating from that sweaty, muscular body, a guttural vindictiveness to his low, raging snorts, that made Rockwall tingle down the back of his neck. Despite the day's chill, his body was already sweating and shiny.

They finally got the tree laced on, the heavy double-rigged Porter that Rockwall had ridden all the way up from Fort Worth. They removed the war bridle and slipped on a heavy, braided hackamore, adjusting it till a cruel pressure could be applied to the big knot under the jaw, bringing it against the tender spot just back of the lower teeth.

Rockwall turned to look at Tie. For a moment he had the impulse to stop the boy, but he knew nothing he could say would do this, and he realized how bad an effect any lack of confidence on his part could have. He stared, tight-lipped, at Tie, fighting back the words. Tie reached for the bars and climbed up to the top, swinging across to put one foot on either side, astraddle above the horse. His face looked pale as he stared down at the beast. As if sensing the moment, Blue Boy had ceased all movement.

It was a branding chute, tighter than a rodeo squeezer, with no room for the rider, and Tie would have to drop into the saddle as the roan came out. Kammas went forward to the gate.

"Yank it," said Tie.

Wood scraped on wood. Big chunks of live, squirming muscle bulged in the roan's rump as it bent those hind legs for the jump-off, and then it was gone, like a jack rabbit, bursting into the open corral with Tie dropping into the saddle. Blue Boy started out like a high roller, bucking straightaway and getting more air between his hoofs and the ground than Rockwall had ever seen before. Then he sunfished and reared up so high Rockwall thought he was going over backward.

"Don't let him hunt those clouds, boy!" squealed Kammas, running down the bars in an ecstasy of excitement. "Knock him down! Knock him down! Look out now! He'll start fence-worming! Don't let him sunfish on you! Give him the can openers, Tie! Here we come, watch that fence, damn' crow-hopper, he's double-shuffling, watch it, watch it . . . !"

Rockwall found he could not stand still, either, and moved down the bars at a restrained pace, bent forward, peering through the heavy pack poles, wincing with every grinding shock Tie took. He had never seen such abandoned savagery in a bucker before. And he had never seen such intelligent, calculating maneuvering. As frenzied as the animal became, it never seemed to lose its judgment of Tie's balance in the leather, fighting to snap him off with a spin, racing for the fence, and wheeling at the last instant in a vicious effort to scrape him away.

The sharp hoofs cut the hard ground to ribbons, and dislodged dirt began to throw its pennants into the air, hiding man and horse for a moment. Then they would burst free once more, jack-knifing, pinwheeling, cavorting madly about the limits of that big pen.

It was the longest space of time Rockwall had ever tried to measure. It had no measure. It seemed an eternity. It could have been only a few minutes.

No man could have taken a beating like that long. Few horses could have kept going at such a pace without folding up. But Blue Boy was still bucking madly when Tie began to show the strain. He miscalculated a pile-driver, and Rockwall could hear his sick grunt above all the other sounds as the beast went into the ground with all four legs like ramrods. The horse came out of it and started pioneering, changing directions with every buck. Tie lost a stirrup and had to grab the saddle horn, doubling forward to keep from going off.

"He's going to chuck you, Tie!" shouted Rockwall, unable to contain himself any longer. "Take a dive while you can!"

But the boy fought to regain his oxbow, finally jamming that pointed toe back into the stirrup. If he went now, he still had enough command of his balance to pick a spot for his dive, but if he tried to ride it out any longer, he would be so beaten it would be the horse that picked the time. Yet, grimly and stubbornly, he sought to maintain his balance. Once more around that churned arena, fighting, squealing, grunting, whinnying, with the two men watching helplessly from outside.

Rockwall had a rope in one hand, waiting to jump in and dab it on the horse when Tie dove. He was pacing back and forth down those bars like a tiger in a cage, now making small, pained sounds deeply in his chest, face twisted with the emotional agony this was causing him.

"For God's sake, Tie," he groaned, "take your dive, you can't do it . . . go any longer and he'll pitch you right into this fence. . . ."

When it came, it was so fast Rockwall missed it. All he knew was Tie clung to the animal one moment and the next was in the dirt, hitting hard and rolling stiffly. With a shout, Rockwall jumped through the bars, loop spinning to keep the horse from trampling the boy. But Blue Boy, seeing he was free of the man, wheeled over toward the far side of the corral and trotted back and forth from one corner to the other, bugling angrily as he studied that barrier too high for him to leap.

"Let's get this boy out of here quick," said Rockwall. "He's beat up bad."

They had to carry Tie through the bars. He was bleeding at the ears and nose, and retching heavily, and could not speak. They carried him over to a water trough by the barn, where Rockwall dipped his own kerchief and washed his face off and gave him water to drink. Sitting on the ground against the trough, Tie threw his head back till he was looking up at the sky, and shook it from side to side in agony that went deeper than his physical pain.

"I ain't never seen a bucker like that," he said. "I ain't never topped anything before like that in my life. God, I ain't . . ."

"That's all right, boy," said Rockwall. "He'll never have a better man step on him, either. We'll get you up to the house now."

They got him as far as the porch. There he pushed them off and dropped into a chair, head in his hands. Something shook his shoulders, and Rockwall sensed the raging disappointment in the boy. "That's that for a while, isn't it?" he asked.

"You and the roan both need a rest," said Rockwall. "Kammas and I will put him back in the stall and give him a couple of days to think things over. He wasn't ready yet. Maybe in another week . . ."

"The hell with that," said Tie, voice cracking. "I'll ride him, and I'll do it the next time you bring the bastard out. I'll ride him till his belly is dragging the dust and he licks my hand and begs me to stop!"

Rockwall studied the boy, then nodded, dropping a significant glance Kammas's way. The old man followed him at a hurried limp down the steps and across the compound.

"Think he's all right to leave alone?"

"I think he wants to be left alone," Rockwall told him.

"Takes it pretty hard," said Kammas.

"He's this way every time he can't ride one out," Rockwall murmured. "I've never seen him take it quite so big, though. I guess that roan has come to be about the most important thing in all our lives."

Chapter Twelve

They got the roan back into the barn with a big fight. Then Rockwall went to saddle up his chestnut and work her. He was in the barn, throwing the kak on her when he became aware of the smell. Its vague familiarity disturbed him, somehow, stirring strange things in him. Suddenly he realized what it was. Aldis's perfume. He turned from the chestnut to see her standing there, studying him in a strange, somber way.

"Will you saddle up Dominoes?" she asked him.

"See Tie?" he said.

"I saw him." There was something petulant in her voice.

"This isn't a very good time to step out on him, Aldis."

"He wanted to be left alone," she said.

He did not answer and went down to the stall for her Appaloosa. Throwing a tie rope on the animal and putting the free end through a ring in the aisle, he went into the tack room for her light-weight Menea. Aldis was fidgeting nervously in the aisle, running a slim hand up and down her braided quirt.

He threw her Navajo blanket onto the horse and loaded the kak on top of this, drawing the latigos through the cinch rings unhurriedly. He could see how his indifferent silence irritated her. Finally she could stand it no longer.

"Well," she said, turning on him. "Why don't you say it?"

"Say what?" he asked.

"I told you so," she said. "That's what you're thinking."

"All newly married couples have their adjustments to make, Aldis."

"That's not what you're thinking."

"I'm trying very hard to mind my own business."

"Well, don't." She came around to him until she stood close, at his shoulder, her face a haunting cameo in the gloom, staring up at him. "Tell me what's really on your mind, Rockwall. Say I'm no good for Tie and you knew from the first this is what would happen. Tell me I'm just a spoiled little rich girl and I haven't got the guts to stick it out on a job like this."

He tugged the latigo tight with a muttering grunt. "That's not what's on my mind at all. I feel sorry for you. You thought all you had to do was get out from under Black Jack's thumb and you could have anything you wanted. And now you find it's not that way at all. Marriage is an obligation on both sides."

"Oh, don't be so unctuous," she said, turning away sullenly. The motion brought her hip, against him, warm, resilient. He shifted away in a vague disturbance. She turned back with the sullenness gone, her voice soft and husky. "Do you really feel sorry for me, Rockwall?"

"Yes," he said uncomfortably, unable to define the strange disturbance in him, or afraid to define it.

"You do, don't you?" she almost whispered, coming so close the whole length of her body pressed against his arm and shoulder. "You understood before. You can see how lonely it gets for a girl up here. Weeks on end, Rockwall, when I don't even see him. In so late I'm asleep and up so early I can't even have breakfast with him. Out there on the Strip running those wild ones or down here bucking himself to pieces eighteen hours a day. I haven't been to Hellgate in a long time, Rockwall. I haven't seen anybody outside for weeks. You talk about obligation. What's the husband's obligation? This isn't marriage. A woman wants to see her man, Rockwall. A woman needs love . . ."

He had turned to face her, and it brought her up against the front of him, pressing him back against the Appaloosa. The horse shifted beneath the pressure, and Rockwall's grab for her arms, to regain his balance, was instinctive. Maybe he pulled her on in, after that, or maybe she mistook the gesture, he would never know, but he did know that the disturbance inside him was clearly recognizable now. He could no longer avoid defining it, as recognizable as it had been that first time they kissed, and he could no more withstand it now than he had then.

For a long, measureless space, the only sound in the barn was the small, muttering shift of animals in their stalls, a vagrant snort, the scrape of a pawing hoof. Then he pulled away, staring at her with a contorted face. Her eyes were half closed, and the smile on her lips held a dreamy triumph. He was still staring at her that way, holding her arms, mind blank with the enormity of it, when a figure was silhouetted in the big door at the end of the aisle.

"Well," said Tie. "Having a little talk?"

There were no longer the extensive green avenues climbing the slopes of the Garnets. They were hushed, white aisles now, between the rows of snow-laden pine. The streams that were not yet frozen over pushed at the ice on their banks with a constant, subdued crackling. On either side of the road fallen trunks lay like bleached bones on an alabaster shore.

Rockwall rode through it all with little notice, his mind on what had happened back there at the barn. He could not tell if Tie had seen him kissing Aldis. The boy had given no evidence of it, although there had been an undertone of irony to his voice. There had been little to say afterwards. Rockwall had finished saddling the Appaloosa and Aldis left, and then he had gone to get the chestnut. He had hoped to find some cattle out here with which to work the horse at cutting. The Forked Tongue ran a drift fence along the ridge above, and there were bound to be a few cuts of beef in the more sheltered spots. But he could not bring his mind to it. He let the chestnut pick her way down the old logging road free-bitted, Aldis still haunting him.

It was no use trying to deny his desire for her. He had felt it too obviously, too vividly. He had been helpless before it, had just taken her in his arms and kissed her without even trying to fight it. It was a despicable thing. His best friend's wife. It left him nothing but bitter disgust for himself. Yet the disgust was one thing and the desire another, and all the disgust he could feel would not dissipate the desire a bit. He knew that sense of torture, again, a squirming, writhing thing inside him seeking escape and finding no way out.

Was that why he hadn't wanted her to marry Tie in the first place? Aldis had said it herself. Jealousy. Yet, he hadn't known it then, hadn't recognized it. No, it couldn't be. He didn't want her for himself. Anything between him and Aldis couldn't last a month. He knew that. His mind knew it. Yet his body didn't. If she came to him again that way . . . No. He shook his head violently with the negation of it. He couldn't do it again. Not to his best friend. And yet, all the time he was telling himself this, something else, something deeper was saying, yes, he could, he could.

The movement down off the slope stopped the maddening whirl of thoughts. At first he thought it was the cattle he sought, and turned the chestnut automatically toward it. Then he saw it was a rider, pushing up through the sere cottonwoods of a creek bottom. There was something familiar about the nervous, stockinged black the man rode, as he picked his way carefully around the deeper drifts to work up toward this road.

Then Rockwall realized why the horse was familiar, and halted his chestnut along the line of trees that shielded him from the man, halting at last on the lip of a coulée where he figured Graves would come out. A tall growth of chokeberry screened him here. The labored breathing of the black began to reach him. He leaned forward and pulled down the noseband on the chestnut to keep him from whinnying. Hoofs breaking through the snow crust sent a soft crunching into the still air. Then the horse gave a huge grunting wheeze, scrambling out of the gully and onto the road. As soon as its head appeared from behind the brush, it shied from the chestnut.

It was not completely out of the gully and almost slid back in. Graves had a battle to keep it upright, and finally brought it onto a level, wheeling to face Rockwall with anger and surprise in his face. His eyes flickered down Rockwall's open Mackinaw to the half-concealed gun at his hip. Graves settled into the saddle then, and his glance climbed back up to lock with Rockwall's.

"Aren't you taking the long way to our place?" Rockwall asked.

"I heard you got the roan," Graves said. "When I want him, I'll come after him."

"Why not admit you were on your way to our place?" Rockwall asked.

Graves's jowls bunched. "I know every move you've made since you caught Blue Boy. I know he hasn't been topped yet, and I'll know when he is topped. I'll come up to see you then, and you'll damned well know it."

Rockwall realized what the man said was true. Graves must have known every move they had made up here. Rockwall was filled with a sense of futility.

"If you did get Blue Boy, what good would he do you?" he asked.

Graves smiled. "If you're talking about the so-called marriage between Tie Taylor and Aldis, that don't mean a thing. If I had that blue roan, Jennings would give me anything I wanted."

Rockwall could not contain his angry reaction. "You can't just pass a woman back and forth like she was a sack of oats."

"Why not?" Graves bent toward Rockwall, voice growing sibilant. "A man would give a lot for that woman, Rockwall, and don't try to tell me you don't appreciate that. She does the same thing to a man that horse does . . . only more so. Tie couldn't stand against it. He's done something for her he wouldn't do for any other reason in the world . . . he's put his pride up for ante. I lost that kind of pride a long time ago, Rockwall. But I'll have something to offer Jennings that'll be worth a lot more."

"You're right . . . when you compare Aldis with the horse," Rockwall said. "She's like the roan in a lot of respects. No man has ever owned either of them. But you still miss the point. We've got the roan in a pen, but he still doesn't belong to us any more than the moon does. The girl belongs to Tie."

"She'll belong to me," Graves said thinly.

"I guess I misjudged you," Rockwall said. "I didn't think you and Jennings were that much alike. He thinks he owns a thing when he's beat it so much it won't fight back."

Graves's voice raised, and it shook a little. "I said she'd belong to me."

"You underestimate Aldis."

"And maybe you underestimate me." Graves was bent toward him again. "I know what's on your mind, Rockwall. You think I'm remembering how you got Laroque and Stanak, and that's why I won't pull on you. When the time comes, you'll get put out of this game. I'm having that blue roan and I'm having Aldis."

"If letting you get that roan means putting Aldis in your hands, you'll never get the roan from me, Graves."

Graves seemed to lift up, nostrils fluttering with a stertorous breath. For a moment, Rockwall thought the man would go for his gun. He

162

guessed the marriage between Aldis and Tie had hurt Graves more than he wanted to admit. Then Graves caught up his reins in a vicious gesture, making the horse dance.

"I'll get Blue Boy, Rockwall. You won't stand in my way."

He wheeled the animal as he spoke, till his back was toward Rockwall. Both his hands were on the reins and his body blocked them off from Rockwall. But Rockwall saw the right elbow twitch. He knew it was too late for his own draw, and jabbed spurs to the chestnut. Graves was just swinging back, left arm lifting so he could shoot from under that elbow, when the chestnut crashed into his horse.

The shock almost unsaddled him, and his gun went off skyward. The chestnut had struck the black on one flank and tried to veer away. Graves tried desperately to retain his seat and line up his gun. Rockwall left his own stirrups in a dive for the man. Graves quit trying to keep his seat, and let his own tilted position carry him off the horse.

Rockwall struck the empty saddle on his belly and slid on over, headfirst, following Graves down. The other man hit on a shoulder and tried to roll aside, but Rockwall's heavy body came against him from above.

Rockwall heard the man's breath leave him with the shock. Dazed himself from hitting so heavily, he pawed for that belly gun. Graves whipped the weapon at him. It tore through his hands and smashed into his face.

Rockwall heard his own hoarse cry. But he caught the man's wrist with both hands and lunged against it, twisting it as he did so.

"Damn you!"

The words left Graves in a shrill gust. Rockwall sensed the hand opening beneath him, and had a dim glimpse of the gun dropping into snow. But he had sacrificed the advantage of being on top.

Graves lashed a leg out and used it as leverage to come up into Rockwall's side. Rockwall's weight was on that wrist and he could not keep from being knocked sprawling. He let go the wrist and allowed himself to flop as far as he could. Graves lunged to his feet, cast one glance for the gun, lost in the snow, and then came at Rockwall.

Rockwall was up on his knees when Graves reached him. He lunged forward into the man, trying to block him. But Graves's rushing weight carried him over backward with his face buried against the sweaty stink of the man's bearskin coat. They rolled over and over down the slope, crashing into blackened timber, plowing through snowbanks, till they finally brought up in a cracking chokeberry thicket. Graves was on top. He came into Rockwall with a blow that almost broke him in two.

Rockwall jackknifed with the pain. He saw

Graves lunge up to strike again, and knew another blow would finish him. He tangled his feet in the man's legs and twisted over with a heaving jerk. Graves was spilled over, and he fell into Rockwall again.

The thicket gave with their combined weight, and once more they were rolling down the slope. Rockwall had a full realization of the man's strength now. That one blow had left him sick and feeble, and he could not bring up enough force to break the man's grip. Dimly, as they flopped over and over through the snow, he knew he would have to finish it this next time or get finished himself.

Finally they smashed into a tree near the bottom. He let himself go completely limp, as if stunned. Graves relinquished his grappling hold and scrambled erect. He lifted a foot to stamp into Rockwall's face.

Rockwall's arms lashed out, catching the foot. Graves spilled, with a surprised shout. Rockwall lunged into the man as he went down. He sank his fist in Graves's belly. Graves doubled up, hugging himself in agony. Rockwall mashed a blow at his face.

It knocked Graves's head back. Rockwall poised his fist again. Graves had enough consciousness left to try to block a second blow to his face. His upraised arm left his belly open once more. That was where Rockwall struck.

Graves's arm dropped. Rockwall hit his exposed face. Graves made a sick, mewing sound and quit trying to block, striving to roll over in a last effort to escape.

Rockwall rolled him back and hit him again and again and again, till the man was completely limp beneath him. Then he crawled away and sagged down against a tree, too drained for any more movement.

He stared dully up the slope, seeing the broken line of their passage down through snow and undergrowth, realizing the whole thing had actually not lasted very long. He did not think he had ever seen so much violence packed into such a short space of time. He felt as though he could never move again. That blow Graves had given him seemed to have torn his belly apart inside.

He finally found the strength to wipe the blood off his face and wash feebly at the slash with fresh snow. Then he found his neckerchief, half torn from his neck, and dabbed at the wound till the blood began to clot. By now Graves was stirring feebly. He groaned and rolled over. His eyes squinted tightly with pain. It took him a long time to gain full consciousness. Then he sat up. One eye was so puffed out he could not open it. He circled the slope with the other till he found Rockwall.

He looked at Rockwall for a long time. There was a sullen anger in his cut and bruised face for a while, but that faded. When he finally spoke, the words were hardly intelligible, leaving his smashed lips in a slurred mumble.

"You cut a bigger plug than I thought."

"And can chew it," said Rockwall.

"This doesn't finish it."

"I know."

"Why didn't you kill me while you had the chance?"

"I suppose you would have?"

"Damn right!" Graves continued to stare at him. Then he started to rise. He moved with great difficulty. Finally, on his feet and swaying there, he looked at Rockwall again, shaking his head. "I guess we live in different worlds." He waited for Rockwall's answer, and, when none came, he took a heavy breath and started to climb the slope. He went to his knees after two steps. He caught at a tree, holding himself erect, and turned to look over his shoulder. Through the bloody mask of his face a frown was visible, as if he were still trying to understand Rockwall. "What in hell will you get out of this, Rockwall, if you do finish it?" he said.

Again Rockwall did not answer. Graves turned and continued on up the slope. But Graves's words were going through Rockwall's mind now. It was as if he could see himself from Graves's viewpoint, and it filled him with a savage, ironic humor. Just what would he get out of it?

This made him realize how subtly and

insidiously he had been sucked into this thing, rebelling at each step, yet forced to take it by one circumstance or another, till he was as deeply involved as all the others, without standing to realize the obvious gain any of them would if they won. And yet, going back to each time he had been more deeply involved, he realized how constantly Aldis had figured in it.

Perhaps this was the one fundamental fact he had to face. Perhaps it was why he had stayed all along. There was no use avoiding it any longer. It was too patent every time they met. He knew a momentary disgust with himself that he could feel such desire for the wife of his friend. Then he knew how foolish that was. A man couldn't help what he felt; he didn't have that much control over his emotions. It was what he did about them that counted. So what would he do? Leave? Would that solve anything? He couldn't let Blue Boy fall into Graves's hands, or Jennings's. He couldn't sell the horse out like that.

Turn the horse loose, then. That was the obvious solution. His own desire for the beast rebelled at that. He swallowed it, realizing that turning the horse loose was not the complete answer. Where would that leave Aldis? Then get her out of it, too. It surged up so strongly that he got completely to his feet with it. Let the horse go and take Aldis and get out.

Then his shoulders slumped again, as he saw

the inevitable result of that. Tie wouldn't take it sitting down. With his hot head, he'd come after them with a gun. And Rockwall had no justification for perpetrating something like that. He would never forgive himself if he had to kill the boy over something of that sort. The more he tried to solve the problem, the more complex it became, until he was all knotted up inside.

He made his way slowly, painfully back up to the chestnut and got aboard, trying to put it all out of his mind. There was one question that came back to him when he blotted out all the others, however. What had Graves been doing up here?

Rockwall watched Graves, riding away, till he was out of sight. Graves certainly hadn't been coming from the direction of Hellgate Strip. Kammas had mentioned one of Jennings's old line cabins up this way, little used now since the bulk of the Forked Tongue herd had been moved into the lower winter pastures. It was located overlooking Black Rock Cañon. Prodded by something he could not name, Rockwall turned the chestnut off the slope.

The road itself had been comparatively free of snow, since the heavy falls had not yet begun, but down here the drifts were deeper, and he went in several times up to his knees, misjudging his path. Finally he reached the creek bottom at the bottom of Black Rock Cañon, and could back-track Graves's trail more easily.

It led down the bottom of the cañon until timber closed completely, and then pulled out onto a shelf on the rim. The shack stood on this shelf, blackened with age, a fallen pole corral flanking it. The door sagged on leather hinges, and there were signs of a horse having stood for some time before it.

Rockwall dismounted, taking off that right glove again and thrusting his hand into the Mackinaw. No sound came from within.

He stepped through the doorway gingerly. The single room was empty. The usual bunks were against the rear wall, filled with moldy straw. The broken hurricane lamp on the rickety table was warm yet. Mingled with the foul odor of that straw was another, fainter scent. Trying to place it, Rockwall heard the noise outside. As he stepped to the door, he realized what the other scent was.

Tie had come up over the shelf, and, when he saw Rockwall, he halted his horse, stepping off. "Everybody sure took out quick," he muttered.

"You didn't seem to want conversation in the barn," said Rockwall.

Tie shrugged. "I'm sorry, Del. I guess I'm getting awfully touchy. I just don't like to be talked about behind my back that way."

"What way?"

"The way you and Aldis were talking there. About me. Oh"—he waved away what he must have thought was Rockwall's protest—"don't try to deny it. You looked as guilty as kids caught stealing watermelons. A man doesn't like to be treated like a child, Del."

"All right, Tie," said Rockwall, swept with a great relief. "I'm sorry."

"Forget it."

"You didn't follow me just to straighten that out," said Rockwall.

Tie shook his head miserably. "I got back to the house and started thinking about how silly it was for me and Aldis to fuss that way. I was going on down to the Forked Tongue and try and catch her there and make it up, when I caught sight of you coming here. What is it?"

Rockwall drew in a breath. "Nothing. I came here to see if Black Jack had a man in this old line shack who could tell me where some cattle were I could use to work the chestnut with. I guess they don't use the place any more."

Tie's hesitation was noticeable. Then he turned and plodded back to his horse. Rockwall took a deep breath, closing the sagging door on its rotting leather hinges behind him, with the scent of Aldis's perfume still in his nostrils.

Chapter Thirteen

It was into the next afternoon when Kammas came limping hurriedly into the barn, where Rockwall was again standing and listening to the muted thunder of Blue Boy's protests against his confinement.

"We got company," the old man reported. "Jennings and some of his bunch."

"It had to come," Rockwall said. "I'm surprised Black Jack hasn't showed up sooner."

They went up to the house, watching the riders come up the trail that led from the cañon. They were in single file, with Jennings out in front, Baxter trailing him, with El Potter in the rear. Tie Taylor and Aldis were both inside the ranch house. Jennings hauled up, resting his big bulk on hands crossed over his saddle pommel.

There was a forced geniality in his voice. "I heard you caught Blue Boy."

"Did you?" said Rockwall.

"Hell," said Jennings, "I can hear him kicking up a ruckus in the barn. That's a sound you don't forget, once you hear it."

"Don't bother to get down, Black Jack," Rockwall said. "I like a visit, but not when I'm busy,"

Jennings was still in his saddle, eyes small and hot with his instant choleric anger. "You telling me I'm not welcome on my own land?" demanded Jennings. "Why, damn you, I set you up here, and I can tear you down and kick you out."

"You set Tie and Aldis up here," corrected Rockwall. "I had a camp that wasn't on your land. I can move back to it pretty quick."

"No!" said Jennings, obviously with the thought that, if Rockwall went, the roan would go with him. "I spoke too quick, Rockwall. But, damn it, so did you! There can't be any hurt letting me have a look at him."

"Jennings," said Rockwall, "I told you once that, if I ever got that roan, there'd be an opportunity to bid for him. When you see me riding him down to the Forked Tongue, you'll know the time has come to talk business."

Jennings looked around at Baxter and Potter. They had changed position a little, edging up toward him. The rancher shifted his big bulk in the saddle.

"I don't like talk that sounds like one thing and means another," he growled. "You've got Blue Boy and he's been giving you one hell of a fight. The way to handle his kind is to hammer his head till he's got blood in his eyes. But you'll never work a horse that way, Rockwall."

"I would!" said Baxter, pale eyes shining. "Snub him tight and wear a set of spurs down to the shank before you ever turn him loose for a ride."

For the first time, Rockwall noticed that Jennings was wearing his gun. Rockwall took a pair of backward steps, with the feeling that he had underestimated the man. Jennings grinned thinly.

"If you won't work that horse the way I want, I'll take him down to the Forked Tongue . . . ," he said. Jennings stopped talking, with a look of frustrated fury replacing his grin. Rockwall risked turning his head and saw Kammas on the cabin porch. The old man's Sharps was lined directly at Jennings's paunch. Jennings swung to the right in his saddle, as if unable to contain his rage. But Baxter was too far away. He swung the other way, face purple, and lashed out an arm as soon as he saw that Potter was within reach. It smashed the man in the face, knocking him clear off his startled horse.

"Why in hell did you let him get the drop on you?" bawled Jennings. "What in hell do I hire you for, anyway?"

Potter rolled over, wiping blood and dirt off his face with a grinding swipe of his hand. "I didn't see him."

"Shut up," Jennings snarled, turning back to Rockwall. Potter rose, licking his mashed lips, and Rockwall saw the venomous hate turn his eyes yellow. Rage vented, Jennings settled into the saddle like a sulking bull. "Damn it,

Rockwall," he said, "make that old devil put down his cannon. We can make a deal."

"No," said Rockwall. "I don't think we can. Not after this. We're breaking Blue Boy and we're gentling him. Until that's over, you won't get your hands on him. Now start riding."

"Five thousand dollars," snapped Jennings. "Cash in your hand. You can have it in the morning as soon as the bank opens at Hellgate."

"Get going."

The baffled anger rose in Jennings again to turn his jowls purple. Kammas shook his rifle a little, suggestively, and the big man wheeled his horse. He dug in his spurs viciously, and the animal squealed, going down the trail in a galvanic burst of speed. Baxter and El Potter swung in behind him.

Kammas lowered the Sharps and brought out his plug of chewing twist. He worried it with his worn teeth, looking at Rockwall speculatively.

"I think that done us both good," he mumbled. "But maybe we knocked down one piece of trouble only to raise up another one."

Rockwall nodded. "Graves already knows we have the roan."

"What'll we do?"

Rockwall shook his head, eyes squinted at the ground with his effort to find a way clear. "If things break right, we'll have a few more days. Maybe the roan will crack."

"You really think so, Rockwall?"

Rockwall glanced up at the shrewd speculation in the old man's eyes. Then he wheeled savagely and stalked away from the house. He wanted to be alone, to try to clear things up for himself. There were so many conflicting patterns of greed and jealousy and desire surrounding the horse. He walked moodily around the corral.

Chapter Fourteen

Tie rode Blue Boy again on Monday, and failed. And Tuesday. And failed. Rockwall made him lay off till Friday, but could restrain the boy no further. It didn't last very long that day, and Tie cracked a handful of ribs coming off. They got him up to the house and Kammas rode for the doctor in Hellgate. The doctor said Tie wasn't too bad, would have to stay in bed for a few days, but warned him against topping any green ones for a long time. Aldis was in the room, and Rockwall left soon, driven by that torture within him.

They had left the roan in the big pen with the kak still on, and Rockwall found himself pulled in that direction. He leaned against the bars, staring through at the big blue beast, trotting restlessly back and forth, and he found the sight blotting Aldis from his mind with something else. Then Kammas was behind him, coming from somewhere.

"You ain't going to do it, Rockwall."

"Do what?" said Rockwall, still absorbed.

"It's been working at you a long time now," said Kammas. "Ever since the kid took his first dive, you been watching the Blue Boy that way. You can't let it get you, Rockwall. If Tie can't top him, I don't think anybody can. You told me once, now I'm telling you. We're too old for the rough string. Especially the worst one in all that string."

It struck Rockwall what the man was driving at, and it struck him with double the force that Kammas was right. It had been in his mind, away down inside somewhere, pulling him like this, prodding him on without his realizing it. Perhaps the inner conflict over Aldis had kept it submerged, but now what Kammas said put it suddenly into focus.

"There's something fascinating about him, isn't there?" he said, staring at the animal. "Something so terrible it pulls you right in, like a bird with a snake, knowing it's deadly all the time and yet not being able to resist it. I wondered why Tie felt so bad about being chucked. He never took on quite so much with any other broomtail. Now I'm beginning to understand. It's what got us all, Kammas. Look at Jennings. An obsession, he said once. Maybe it is. And Graves. Willing to kill for it. And you, out there five years, waiting for your chance. Nobody who sees him forgets him, and any horseman who catches sight of him is caught in it. Not his physical appearance, so much. I've seen horses as beautiful. Something inside. His spirit. Those eyes. His movement. Like a beautiful woman you can't leave alone. We're wound up with that horse, Kammas, and, if one of us can't finish it, the next one has to, one way or the other."

"No, Rockwall." Kammas clutched his arm. "He'll bust you wide open and spill your sand all over the ground. Your bones aren't as green as a kid's. They'll crack like dry kindling. Tie can get away with it, but you'll . . ."

"How has Tie taken his fall every time?"

"From the horse to the ground. How else is there? It's happened too fast to watch."

"I lost it the first time," said Rockwall. "But I've been catching it since. Ever see a horse do that pump-handle pile-driver the way this roan does?"

"I've never seen a horse do anything the way this roan does."

"Or as long," said Rockwall. "Another animal would come to pieces under a pounding this roan gives. That's the spot to watch, Kammas. He stays in the pump handle so long Tie gets fuzzy. He knows just when to switch from the pump handle to sunfishing. Tie's so dazed he loses the switch and he's off. But if a man was watching for that sunfishing . . ."

"Rockwall, please"—there was a moaning plea to the old man's voice now—"so it would take you to figure it out like that. All the figuring in the world won't help here. That horse just wasn't meant to be rid."

"I don't think I'll know any peace till I try, Kammas," said Rockwall. "You were right. It's got me. I don't sleep good nights. When I do sleep, I dream. You can understand it. You've been running these animals all your life. Only a man who talks their language would understand the grip one like this can get on you. Come out and help me get him in the chute."

The old man's arm slipped off as Rockwall stooped through the bars. He took a coiled dally off the top rail and walked toward Blue Boy. The horse began to snort and wheel. Rockwall tried to maneuver him into the corner. The horse escaped and charged across the corral.

"Get out of there, you fool." Kammas squealed at him. "He'll trample you alone."

"Come help me, then," said Rockwall. "I'm getting him into that chute, with or without you."

Cursing in three Indian tongues, the old man ducked nimbly through the poles. Between them they finally fought the animal into that chute, closing the door. Then Rockwall climbed up on top. When he nodded, Kammas jerked the gate open once more. Rockwall knew Blue Boy was wise to the squeezer now, and would probably wheel right or left as soon as he was free in an effort to escape Rockwall's drop mount. It was left, and he spun almost before his rump was free. But Rockwall had expected it, and threw the weight of his body that way so he was leaning far out to the left when he struck the saddle.

Blue Boy's feel for the rider's balance was uncanny. Feeling the man coming into the tree that way, he changed his leads before Rockwall was completely onto the saddle, and wheeled off to the other side. Rockwall threw his weight the other way, jabbing his sharp-toed boots for the oxbows at the same time. Feeling that change of weight, Blue Boy once more reversed his field, rearing up this time.

With only one foot in the stirrup. Rockwall could not have matched this shift if the horse had whirled instead of rearing. But the lift threw him forward against the saddle horn instead of off to the side, and, although it knocked the air out of him, he got his other foot into the wood.

He straightened up, ready for the next one, and now it was the grind, riding it out till the roan went into its final act, that pump-handle piler. Back and forth, around and around, up and down. The pattern of poles shifting and plunging about him. The dirt funneled up in a miniature cyclone or fanned into russet pennants or thrown into his face in a choking puff. The smell of sweat and blood and dirt and lather. The squeal of the animal. The whinny. His own husky shouts. His sounds of pain.

Then, suddenly, he was on that pump handle, the roan hunting clouds and coming down stiff-legged, the hind hoofs hitting before the front, striking ground in a see-saw pile-driver that rocked the man back and forth as though it sought to drive his spine through his hat.

He gave it a slack body, rocking with it, feeling the blood pumping into his head with the force of each shock and knowing it would be streaming from his nostrils in a moment, waiting, waiting for that final switch to throw him off.

He could feel the devilish horse waiting for him to slacken, to gauge one shift of bone and muscle just a little bit wrong. He felt his perceptions going fuzzy, his concentration dissipating, and knew it was coming, knew he could not hold on much longer. And still the horse went up and came down, went up and came down.

"Sun your moccasins, Rockwall, you can't hang on any longer! Let him chuck you now and pick your bed . . . !"

With Kammas's voice in his ears, Rockwall took a final chance, knowing he could not last any longer, and began simulating a loss of balance. When those back hoofs struck, he let himself almost go over the cantle, and, when the fore-hoofs drove into the ground, he let his body lurch over its center of gravity to the front.

It fooled the animal, for, as Blue Boy went up again, his whole, writhing frame seemed to slither out from beneath Rockwall, and the roan was sunfishing. It was what he had been waiting for, and he still had enough perception to catch it.

As the roan twisted his right shoulder into the ground, throwing his belly up at the sun, Rockwall's whole body was twisted down over his left shoulder. And as the maddened horse twisted the other way to throw his left shoulder down and his belly at the sun from the other side, Rockwall was throwing his weight back to counter-balance that.

The roan came out of its sunfishing with a baffled scream, and started pioneering in a mad frenzy all over the corral. But this did not have the calculation that had marked the animal's bucking before, and in that moment, Rockwall had thought he had won. Grunting in agony every time those hoofs struck, he tried to ride it out. The frenzy seemed to abate. It was becoming a crow-hop around the corral. Rockwall felt his whole body starting to relax.

Suddenly he found himself thrown high into the air. Instinct was the only thing that kept him in leather. Then he was coming down again. The pile-driver struck with Rockwall utterly unprepared. He thought the saddle had hit the bottom of his brain. Flashing lights filled his vision. He felt himself rising again. Was he still in the saddle? It caused him actual physical agony to bring his mind into focus, to force his body slack for that next pile-driver. Front and back they hit, jerking him over the cantle, and then pulling him forward onto the horn with stunning force. He had enough clarity left to know this was the end. He could not hope to last until Blue Boy started sunfishing again. If he didn't take his dive now, the horse would do the choosing and pitch him like a sack of sand.

He let the roan hunt for those clouds again. At the peak, he shifted his weight to roll off, picking a spot free of the fence. When they struck again, he was completely limp, his body angled so that the jar took him off and rolled him into the ground. He stopped himself before he was brought up against the fence, and got to his knees and scuttled out between the bars.

On the outside, he sagged against a pole, unable to support himself longer, even on hands and knees. Blood was streaming from somewhere. His nose? Then he was very sick. Kammas was by him then, but let him alone till the nausea passed. Finally Rockwall hauled himself up till he could look at the roan.

"I would have been disappointed in you if you'd tried to ride him out," said Kammas. "That ain't guts. It's pure stupidity." Rockwall continued to stare at the animal, and Kammas seemed driven to ask it finally, in a husky, reluctant voice that held his own answer to the question he asked. "What do you think, Rockwall?"

"What do *you* think?" said Rockwall sickly.

"I imagine I'm thinking the same thing you are," said Kammas. "I'd trust your judgment first, though, and I wouldn't say that to any other man in the world. I think you've known it from the first time Tie topped the roan, but you had to find out yourself to be convinced."

'You're right, Kammas." Rockwall nodded. "I hoped I was wrong. But I guess I wasn't. I don't think the horse can be broken."

Chapter Fifteen

They went on, after that, but it was not the same, somehow. When Tie could get up and around, he came down to the corrals and stood for hours looking through the bars at the roan. Kammas ran out of tobacco and didn't even ask Rockwall to pick him up some more when he was in town. Rockwall himself was probably in the worst mood of all, although he showed it least. He could not help feeling his own depression, over the horse, or being influenced by theirs. Added to this was the constant, growing conflict within himself about Aldis.

She was around all the time. She seemed to be deliberately taunting him, with the way she dressed, her looks, her movement. She herself was restless, and he wondered how soon again she would leave. It came, finally, when Tie was fairly well healed. Aldis and Tie had a fight over it that evening, and the next morning, when Rockwall came down to the barn, the Appaloosa was gone.

There were probably a lot of motives in him, some he would not face himself. Whatever was driving him, he got out the chestnut and told Kammas he was again going to hunt some cattle toward the east to work the horse with. He rode several miles across their own undeveloped acreage until reaching the Hellgate road. He turned down this toward the juncture with the old logging road. Almost afraid to separate and identify the turgid, mingled emotions stirring in him, he turned up this winding, fading trace into the Garnets.

When he reached the spot, he turned off the road. Again it was that creek bottom, running into Black Horse Cañon, with the timber closing in, and the aged, blackened cabin. The Appaloosa stood before it. He let his rigging *creak* as he stepped off the chestnut.

"Kenny?" called the girl from inside.

"Sorry to disappoint you," he said, stepping into the door.

She stared at him a long time. The pupils of her eyes, large and black at first with the surprise of his appearance, narrowed again, until they held the purring, tawny obliquity of a cat's. "Maybe it isn't such a disappointment," she murmured.

"Aldis," he said. "Why did you marry Tie?"

She drew a deep breath, holding her answer so long he finally thought it would not come. "Maybe I love him," she said finally.

"And Graves, too?" said Rockwall. "Or if it had been Graves you married, would you have gotten tired of him just as quick and started dabbling on the outside with Tie?"

"You would be there, either way, wouldn't you?" she almost whispered.

"I don't think you love either of them," said Rockwall. "Love to you is nothing more than holding them in your arms and kissing them and stringing them along as long as they have the money to entertain you. When the going gets rough, you start looking around for more excitement. Black Jack would have cut you off cold if you had married Graves, wouldn't he? Poor Tie never knew what he put his rope on."

"You always figure things out so clearly," she said. "I suppose you even have some names for me."

"I suppose I do," he said. "But it wouldn't do much good to put them on you. I don't think anything will do you much good."

"Do you also have a name for a man who wants his best friend's wife?"

It was like a slap in the face, and he could not hide its effect. She tilted her head back, and her laugh was so deep it stirred the satiny curve of her throat. It held all the ruthlessness of her.

"So you wanted to sit in judgment," she said.

"I didn't come to do that," he said.

She moved closer. "I'm glad," she said. "I'm glad the air is clear. Now you can meet me on my own terms, Rockwall. Now you won't have to look so tortured when I kiss you. So we're both a couple of tramps. I'm his wife and you're his best friend, and we'll enjoy it all the more for the fact."

"I didn't come to do that, either," he said. "You're going back to him, Aldis. You're not coming here to see Graves any more."

"Sure I'll go back," she murmured. "If you'll be there."

"If I'm there, it won't be for that," he said.

"Oh." There was condescension to her raised brows. "You're just asking me to go back and be good."

"I'm telling you."

"What if I don't?"

"I could horsewhip you through the streets of Hellgate and tell everybody exactly why I'm doing it."

She drew in a thin, attenuated breath, studying him, and then released that chuckling, throaty little laugh again. "You're quite capable of that, aren't you?"

"Yes," he said. "Shall we go?"

She tossed her head, turning restlessly away to pace across the room. "I'm getting tired of this big brother act, Rockwall. Kenny will be here in a minute. You'll be the one who goes."

"I don't want to put my hands on you, Aldis."

"You'll be sorry if you do."

He saw that she would not come, and stepped forward to grab her. He caught one arm, and she let it swing her around into him. The abrupt contact of her body stopped all his movement in that instant. Her free hand clutched the lapel of his Mackinaw. The devil was in her smile.

"Yes, Rockwall?" she said in a soft, mocking way. Then her arm slipped about his neck and she was kissing him again. He pulled his head back, swinging free, crying out in a tortured way.

"No, Aldis, I'm not doing this to Tie again, and neither are you. You're coming back with me, damn you. . . ."

Her hands were locked together. "I've been frantic. Uncle Black Jack's been in a vile temper. The only reason he doesn't ride up with his whole crew and try to take Blue Boy from you is that he knows the roan isn't broken yet. Baxter's tried to tell him they can break the animal themselves, but Uncle isn't convinced. But that isn't what I want to tell you. When the doctor got back to Hellgate and it leaked out that Tie's ribs were broken, people actually began taking bets on how soon Kenny would come up after Blue Boy. Kenny won't see any point in waiting any longer, now that he knows Tie can't break the animal. And do you remember Pedro?"

"The barman who took the pool cue to me that night?"

Aldis nodded. "He's the best man Graves has left, now that Laroque and Stanak are gone. Kenny told me earlier that he's ready to jump. He had Pedro with him. They're on their way now, Rockwall. In fact, I thought it was all over, that Kenny had come back to me, that he has Blue Boy. What are you going to do about that?"

He let his air out in a discouraged breath. "What else is there to do? Try to stop them from getting the horse."

A desperate note entered her voice. "Why does it have to be that way? Pitting your life against Kenny's. Why can't you just turn the horse loose?"

"Do you think I haven't thought of that a million times?" he said in a savage burst. "It wouldn't solve a thing. Jennings would annul your marriage to Tie. Not that it would matter much to you. But it would to Tie. Tie would go off the deep end."

"You didn't let me finish," she said, grasping his arm. "Will you blind yourself to the obvious way out forever? Let the horse go, Rockwall. We'll go with it."

He stared at her, feeling his face tightening up.

She caught his other arm, eyes dark and intense.

"Why not put it in words, Rockwall? It's been in both our minds for a long time now. You can't deny it, can you? I thought I could live up to my bargain with Tie when I made it. Now I know it would be impossible. I tried running away before and it never worked. But you're strong enough to buck Uncle Black Jack, even if he came after us. I know that. Together we could beat him."

"I won't try to deny it's been in my mind, too," he said. "But I couldn't sell Tie out that way. Then there's Graves. It's pretty obvious he'd still be around even if it was me instead of Tie"

She shook her head, tear-filled eyes trying to meet his. "What's Tie donc to deserve your friendship like this? He's like a spoiled child. He's already turning on you. How do you know he isn't already working for Kenny? Look what you're sacrificing in this effort to save Tie. Me, the horse, even yourself. Is Tie worth that? I don't want to hurt Tie any more than you do. I know he isn't basically bad. But he's weak. Maybe part of his weakness is youth. We can't give him time to grow up. We've got to make a choice."

She tried to plaster herself against him again, and this time his efforts to avoid it swung her around against the wall so hard she let out a stunned gasp, and he felt her start sliding toward the floor in his grasp. He had to twist around against her to catch her arms and keep her from falling. At that moment, Tie stepped through the door.

Rockwall turned a strained, twisted face toward the boy. Then he realized how he was holding Aldis, and how it looked, and stepped back. Still stunned, Aldis braced herself against the wall, staring at Tie. Rockwall was surprised, in that moment, to see no fear in her face.

"So you been working the chestnut in Forked Tongue cattle over here," said Tie, barely audible.

Rockwall held out one hand. "Tie . . ."

"I'm really disappointed in myself for not catching on sooner," said the boy through lips that barely moved. "Is this what you were doing in the barn the other day? And I thought you'd just been talking about me. I resented being talked about like I was a kid or something. Talking?" His sound could hardly be called a laugh. Suddenly all the tight-lipped restraint came apart about him, and he jumped for Rockwall, filling the little shack with his choked shouts. "Damn you, Rockwall, god damn you . . . !"

"Tie!" cried Rockwall, jumping back. "Don't! I can't fight you . . . !"

"Then take the beating of your life!" yelled Tie, and hit him in the belly. The blow, and Tie's body crashing on into Rockwall with its forward momentum, knocked him back into the corner. He caught a blurred glimpse of the woman's face beyond, filled with an eager, savage light, as she bent forward to see this, and he realized it was no vindication or revenge that excited her so, but the mere sight of seeing them fighting.

Then Tie was hitting him again in the belly, in the ribs, in the face. Stiffened against the wall by the blows, his whole body jerked with the instinctive impulse to block and counter punch. His arms flew up in the first part of it, fending off the boy's next blow. But he just couldn't strike back somehow, he just couldn't hit the boy.

He could hear the explosive sound his breath made leaving him. He could feel the wall against his back, or the floor, and then his hands were filled with splinters, and he must have clawed his way back again. Pain was only comparative. There were the great spasms of it, with each blow, and the hurt in between that didn't last long enough to gain separate identity before the next blow.

"Tie," he heard himself saying, in a choked, feeble way, "Tie . . . Tie . . ."

Faces spun before him and a fist blotted that out. He was doubled over, spitting something red. The whole room was filled with shooting, flashing lights. He couldn't see any more. His eyes were wet. His whole being seemed jerked this way and that by some jarring impacts. He heard an incoherent, animal sound come gutturally from deeply within himself. He heard someone else grunt, and again his consciousness seemed to lift and expand, and then burst with that impact of something.

"Tie," he kept saying, over and over again, "Tie, Tie, Tie . . ."

He let the mumbled words trail off. He realized he was huddled in a heap against the junction of two walls and the floor. The pain no longer came in those blasting spasms. It was dull, throbbing, filling his whole being. Sight returned fuzzily. He made out the table, upset, with the hurricane lamp smashed to bits in an opposite corner. Then the lighter rectangle of the door. It took him a long time to realize the room was empty. They were gone.

Chapter Sixteen

The storm had broken by the time Rockwall got back. The wind had risen to a howling gale that blotted out all other sounds and the snow was swept down on it, soft and feathery at first, to thicken till its weight whipped against timber and slope with shaking force. Rockwall's whole body was numb with chill and battering when he at last drove the staggering little chestnut through growing drifts to see the dim pattern of corral poles through the falling snow. He turned and the horse ran heavily against the barn.

He got off, almost going to his knees, and struggled with the door. He had to haul the animal in, and only then did he realize there was a light inside. Kammas was coming up to him and saying something.

"Wind's knocking the barn so hard I didn't even hear you."

He helped Rockwall close the door and off saddle the chestnut and rub him down and blanket him. The old man had built a fire in the small Franklin stove they kept in the tack room. Kammas stopped with Rockwall at the door, staring at his cut face.

"Tie?" the old man said.

"He found Aldis and me together." Rockwall drew a long breath. "Maybe I deserved it."

"Man can't help what he feels, Rockwall," Kammas said. "I knowed you was in love with that girl first time I saw you look at her. I also knowed you wouldn't cross Tie as long as he was in love with her."

"I guess he wasn't that sure," Rockwall said wryly.

"He must have had something in his mind," Kammas said. "He got restless pretty soon after you left. When he took out, I figured he was tailing you."

"He saw us one time in the barn," Rockwall said. "It must have put something at the bottom of his mind, and he started adding things up. He must have remembered about that old line cabin where he found me that other time. Funny part of it was, I hadn't gone out to meet Aldis this morning. I didn't even know for sure she was there. She was waiting for Graves, not me. Aldis said Graves has pulled Pedro off the bar. I think Tie'll be in on it, too, now. That'll be three, at least. Tie and Aldis are probably with him by this time. The way Aldis talked before Tie got there, I had the idea Graves and Pedro were already on their way here to get Blue Boy . . ."

His voice trailed off. Kammas was looking down the aisle. Both of them seemed drawn by the same thing. They began to walk back, until they stood before the roan's stall. The blue beast was pawing hay and shifting nervously around in the small space, emanating that same sense of latent violence with his slightest motion, the bunched muscles jumping and rippling beneath the sheen of his hide, the nostrils flaring defiantly. He met their gaze, eyes rolling white as china, backing up against the rear wall. The barn was filled with the sullen, battering sound of the storm, joists and rafters squeaking in a muted obbligato to the constant shudder of the sides and roof.

"So Graves is coming after you, Blue Boy," murmured the old man, gazing at the horse. There was a strange, soft light in his eyes. He turned to Rockwall. "If Graves wasn't coming, and there wasn't no storm, what would be on your mind?"

Rockwall was silent a long time, hating to say it. "He's beat us fair and square, Kammas. Don't you think he deserves his freedom now?"

Kammas turned away, clearing his throat uncomfortably. "I guess that's what's been in both our minds since that time you tried to ride him."

"Where do you suppose the wild ones go in the Strip when a storm like this hits?"

"They've got their hide-outs," said Kammas. "Nothing around here that would give Blue Boy protection, though. I'd say turn him out now rather than take a chance of Graves's getting him, but Blue Boy don't know this country. The storm might pull him down."

"That's what I thought," Rockwall murmured. "But the storm'll be over sometime, and Graves won't get him."

"Not 'less he gets me first," Kammas said thinly.

The horse quieted an instant, staring at them. Then he turned away, switching his tail. Rockwall and the old man went back to the tack room in a subdued silence, both saddened by the knowledge of this. Rockwall shucked his Mackinaw and Kammas poured him a cup of coffee from the pot he had simmering on the stove. Its heat thawed Rockwall out some.

"Think Graves will wait till the storm's beat itself out?" Kammas asked.

Rockwall shook his head. "He'll know Tie and I are through now. He'll consider the possibility that we mean to turn the horse loose. He'll know we can't do it during the storm. I think Graves'll buck the snow and come up anyway."

"That's a hell of a thing. It'll be a blizzard in a couple of hours. I wouldn't give a man a fifty-fifty chance of getting through."

"It's his last chance, Kammas, you've got to remember that. Graves knows the country as well as anybody. I think he's capable of making it."

"We might have a few hours," Kammas said. "You get some shut-eye and I'll keep watch."

Rockwall took to the bunk beside the stove where Kammas had been sleeping for some weeks now. He did not think he would be able to sleep, but he dropped off after a while with the buffeting of the storm fading from him.

When he awoke, the sounds had ceased. The fire was low, and Kammas was not in the tack room. Rockwall sat up, wincing at the pain of aching muscles. His face, too, was stiff and sore, and his underlip felt swollen. He rose and went to the door. Some vague motion at the other end of the dark aisle caught his attention.

"Kammas?"

"First blow's over," Kammas said from down there. "It'll be quiet a couple of hours. I still think that blizzard's coming, though."

Rockwall walked sleepily down toward the man, rubbing at a shoulder, sore from one of Tie's blows. Most of the animals were quiet, but Blue Boy was moving restlessly in his stall, snorting softly. When Rockwall reached Kammas, he realized the old man had the door open slightly.

It was night. Beneath the bright light of a rising moon, the snow blanketed everything, lying a foot high on the roof of the house, piled in deep drifts against the corral fence. Kammas spoke in a hushed voice.

"Worried about Blue Boy. Them other animals is used to men. Somebody coming without his horse, they wouldn't take much notice. But that roan's more nervous than he ought to be."

"How long've I been asleep?"

"About three hours . . ."

He broke off, staring out into the snow. Rockwall saw it, also. A man, on foot, laboring through the drifts. He was heading toward the house, leaving a deep, weaving trail in the snow. Halfway between barn and house he stumbled, going to hands and knees.

"It's Tie," Rockwall said.

The boy fought to his feet and stumbled on a few more paces, and then went down again. He was sprawled out on his belly in the snow. Rockwall felt his eyes begin to squint with the tension of waiting for the boy to rise. Finally he made an involuntary move.

"Hold it," Kammas advised. "They'd have you on the hip out there."

So they stood there again, with the sullen sounds of the roan in his stall filling the barn. Tie did not move. Rockwall searched the timber beyond the pens vainly for sign of movement.

"We can't let him lie there," he said finally. "He'll freeze to death."

"I'm going to take a look out the other end of the barn," Kammas said. He walked down through the gloom and opened the small back door. At last he came back, the weight of the buffalo gun dragging at each step he took. "Nothing there," he said.

Once more they waited, watching, listening, and Rockwall broke the silence at last. "Keep me covered. I'm going out."

"If they're waiting, they'll have you."

"Timber's too far away for their six-guns," Rockwall said. "Graves is too smart to set up a trap with that much of a chance involved."

He got his Hopkins out anyway, and slid through the door. He was rigid with tension by the time he reached Tie. He knelt, turning the boy over. Tie mumbled vaguely, pawing at Rockwall.

"Gotta get back to Del," he said. "Take me back to the outfit."

"You're back now, kid," Rockwall said.

Tie blinked through the snow hedging his

brows and shook his head wonderingly. "Del," he said feebly. Then he sank back. "Lost my horse a ways back. Thought I'd freeze to death walking through that snow. I'm sleepy, Del."

Rockwall got his hands under the boy's armpits, dragging him back to the barn. It was a great labor through the snow with that dead weight, and he was gasping by the time he reached the barn. Kammas would not leave the door, however, to help Rockwall get the boy into the tack room, so Rockwall left the old man on guard and labored back to the other end with the boy. He stripped him of his boots and snow-crusted Mackinaw and wrapped him in warm blankets. Then he forced hot coffee down him. After the second cup, Tie shook his head groggily.

"What makes me so sleepy?" he said.

"It gets you that way," Rockwall said. "Think you're sleepy when really you're just played out. Go to sleep in the snow and freeze to death. Lucky you reached here before you finished your string."

"Yeah." Tie shook his head again, grinning wryly. Then the grin faded. He was staring at Rockwall. He lifted his hand. "Del . . ."

He stopped, as if unable to find the words he wanted to say. Rockwall saw the plea in his face, helpless and young. It was the same look he had seen there the first time, when Tie had wanted to join him. Rockwall remembered what he had thought then—*if he was a puppy, he'd be wagging his tail.*

"What happened, Tie?" he asked quietly.

Tie shook his head miserably, looking at the floor. "Am I just a plain damned heel, Del?"

Rockwall stood up, still holding the empty coffee cup, and moved restlessly about the room. "No, Tie. I guess I would've felt the same way, if I walked in and found a friend holding my wife in his arms."

"You might have felt the same way, Del. But you wouldn't have beat the hell out of your friend when he was too decent to fight back because he might knock one of your busted ribs through a lung." Tie was squinting up at Rockwall. "You love Aldis, don't you?"

Rockwall shook his head in a tortured way. "That's just it, Tie. I don't think I do. Not really. I kept trying to deny it, even to myself. But now I think I know. It wasn't me, Tie, that Aldis was meeting at that line shack. It was Graves."

"Can't we work it out, Del, now that we understand each other?" Tie asked.

The tone in Tie's voice lifted Rockwall's gaze to his face. Tie's blue eyes were no longer bleary, and there was an expression in them Rockwall had never seen before. It was so obscure he could not read it. Somehow it disturbed him. Tie took a deep breath and got to his feet.

"Would the right way be to let Aldis decide

201

which one of us she really wants?" Tie said.

Rockwall studied him with a wonder shining in his eyes. "You've really grown up tonight, haven't you?"

Tie shrugged uncomfortably. Before Rockwall could speak again, there was a small noise behind him, and he turned to see Kammas coming down the aisle.

"Everything's all right, old-timer," Rockwall said, grinning. "Tie's back with us."

Kammas was unrelenting. "Don't buy a pig in a poke, Rockwall."

Rockwall felt his smile fade a little. "Slack off, Kammas. I told you the kid had sand at the bottom. He just needed time to figure it out."

Tie grinned sheepishly at the old man. "I don't blame you for mistrusting me, Kammas. I guess I've switched ends too many times since you've come here, haven't I?"

"You see any sign of Graves before you turned back?" asked Kammas woodenly.

Tie shook his head. "I was almost to the Forked Tongue. I didn't see anybody on the road into Hellgate."

Kammas frowned. "I can't believe he isn't coming."

"After the horse?" Tie looked from Kammas to Rockwall. Then he laughed. "I wish he would come. I'd just like to see him try and get that roan, against the three of us." He broke off, looking down at the empty holster on his hip. "I'll need a gun, Del. I must have lost mine wandering through the snow."

"I wouldn't give you a toothpick," growled Kammas.

"Take it easy," Rockwall told him. "Tie, you better lie down. If you were falling asleep in that snow, you were more played out than you realized. My saddle gun's up at the house. I'll get it for you."

Tie lay back in the bunk and Rockwall covered him. Then he stirred the fire to a new blaze and stepped outside. Kammas was standing there in the gloom, muttering to himself.

"You sure take a lot of chances with that boy, putting a gun in his hand."

"It could be we'll need his help," Rockwall said. "But I won't do it blindly, Kammas. Not without being sure."

"Damn it, you told him you'd get your saddle gun from the house."

"Where did you put the saddle when you took it off my chestnut?" Rockwall interrupted.

Kammas frowned at him. "Hung it over the top bar between the chestnut's stall and the next."

"My saddle gun's in the boot on that rigging," Rockwall said. "It'll stay there till Tie proves he's back for good."

Kammas stared at him for a moment, then a grin etched its thousand wrinkles into the old man's face. "You damned old fox," he said.

Rockwall gave him an affectionate shove on the shoulder and told him to get back to the other door. Then he turned and walked to the smaller door at the rear, unbarring it to look out. The moon was dropping lower and the shadows lay like black velvet beneath the timber. His eyes began to smart from searching the glaring white fields of snow for movement. He began to get sleepy after a while, and turned back into the tack room for a cup of coffee. He stepped through the door and stopped short at the sight of Tie lying in the bunk, covers up to his chin, unwinking eyes fixed on Rockwall.

"I'm not sleepy now, Del," he said. "Isn't that funny?"

"Yeah." Rockwall went to the stove, poured himself a cup of coffee. "Take it easy anyway. I don't want to leave that door too long. Time's running out."

"Sure is," said Tie.

Rockwall glanced at him again, then took a gulp of the coffee.

"You get me that saddle gun?" Tie went on.

"Not yet," said Rockwall. "A little later."

He turned to go out and had reached the door of the room when Tie spoke again.

"Rockwall."

The quiet tone of it stopped him as if Tie had shouted. He knew a sudden strange reluctance to turn back. "Yeah?" he said, looking around.

"Yeah," Tie answered. Firelight twinkled dully on the nickel plating of the Derringer in his hand. It was so small only the snub-nosed barrel was visible beyond his encircling fingers. "I guess I won't need the saddle gun after all," Tie said. "This was in my Mackinaw pocket all the time. It's one of Kenny's."

Rockwall found his eyes settling helplessly, irrelevantly on the sodden Mackinaw where he had dropped it in the corner. It just hadn't occurred to him to go through it. Then he had the impulse to throw his coffee.

"Don't do that," Tie said. "I'd get you before it hit my eyes. Set the cup down, then take out your Hopkins and put it on that chair over there."

Rockwall did as he was told. He was swept with the nausea of an intense, frustrated rage. Not so much rage at Tie as at his own gullibility. As he took his gun out and set it on the chair, he heard his voice coming out thickly.

"Don't be a fool, Tie. Can't you see how Graves is using you? He couldn't get the horse any other way. What do you hope to gain out of this? Graves wants Aldis as bad as you. He's never stopped wanting her."

"Think I want her . . . now?" The words left Tie like ripping cloth. "Graves can have her. It's been you all along. Aldis admitted that to me at the line shack while you were down and just as

Graves rode up. She had been waiting for you. All I want now is money. A man can go a long ways with five thousand. All I want is the money and seeing you left holding the sack."

"Maybe you want revenge more than the money."

"Shut up, Del." Tie's voice sounded strained. Rockwall could see how tightly his lips lay against his teeth. Tie threw off the blanket, swinging out of the bunk. "Don't shove me any further," he said thinly. "I was close to shooting you at the line shack." He went over to the chair and picked up Rockwall's gun, then called through the open tack room door. "Kammas! I've got Rockwall back here. Drop your gun and come to this end of the barn. Light's strong enough to see you three stalls away from this door. If you've still got your gun when you get there, I'm shooting Rockwall."

Rockwall felt the sweat crawl down his arms beneath his shirt. Kammas came into view, standing stooped and empty-handed in the rectangle of light that the open door of this room threw across the barn. That same light caught opaquely in the glitter of his eyes.

"So you're back with us?" he said thinly.

The feverish light varnished Tie's eyes. "What kind of man would come crawling back to the so-called friend who wanted his wife?" He was looking at Rockwall now. "She wouldn't have got in this if it wasn't for you, Del. She and I would have been all right if you hadn't tried to sit in. Now you've got her so mixed up she don't know which way the kak's turned."

"Mixed up?" Rockwall stared at the boy, seeing it for the first time, the red-rimmed eyes, filled with driven unreasoning rage, the set, fanatical look to the bunched muscles of his jaw. Rockwall tried one last time, holding out his hand in a vague, pleading way. "Tie, don't be a fool . . ."

"That's good advice. I've been a fool too long. I should have shot you today instead of just beating you. I also think you wanted Aldis for yourself . . . have from the beginning. You figured you could ace me out. Aldis admitted as much. She's been with you more times than she ever was with me, and she's never been with Graves. She said it was you she wanted. Graves knows it. That's why he offered me a deal in town. He offered the same deal today, and I took it. But you, Del, you were my pard, and you played me for the fool with her. Aldis is ashamed of what she's done. Of what you made her do. If it hadn't been for you, things could've worked out. Graves only mattered to her when she wanted to get away from Black Jack. That's when you moved in. She couldn't help herself."

"She tell you that?" Rockwall asked.

"Did you ever think that, if Rockwall had wanted to, he could've taken the girl and gone?" Kammas said. "If *she* wanted to go?"

"Shut up, old man." The boy's voice was shrill. "Shut up, both of you. This goes back a long ways. Del couldn't have got Blue Boy alone. So he figured it all out, how he could get the horse and Aldis. He couldn't get Blue Boy without me, so he let me think I'd get Aldis, just to keep me in the game. Then light a shuck with everything! Well, now he won't get anything. Aldis is back with Black Jack and Graves will get Blue Boy and I'll get five thousand dollars."

Kammas shook his head. "You damn' fool! You couldn't have got it more twisted up."

"I said shut up!" Tie's voice cracked as he jerked toward Kammas. Rockwall could see his hand trembling with the Hopkins. Finally Tie turned back to Rockwall and waved him on ahead, out the door.

Rockwall stepped into the aisle, heard Tie come out after him. The boy prodded him toward the smaller door at the rear of the barn. He opened it and fired three times into the night. The echoes rolled out over the ridges and slammed against higher rock faces and came back multiplied. Finally they died, and the silence settled down. Kammas had come out of the tack room, also, and Tie was watching both of them. The boy was in his shirt sleeves now, and he began to shiver in the chill. He stamped his feet. Then the tension in him broke loose.

"Damn it, Graves!" he shouted. "Come on in!"

There was another long space of silence, broken only by muted sounds of sleepy horses in the barn. Kammas caught Rockwall's eye, and Rockwall knew the old man wanted to make some kind of break. But Tie was watching them too closely. Finally the boy jerked the Hopkins at them.

"Get back in the room. It's too damned cold to wait out here."

He herded them back into the tack room and went over to stand by the stove, warming himself there. He bent to pick up his Mackinaw, found it was still too soggy to wear, and got Rockwall's coat off the hook, instead. Then Rockwall heard horses snorting outside, and the *creak* of the outer door opening.

"In here," Tie said irritably. "Why in hell did you wait so long?"

Graves appeared in the doorway, his heavy body appearing even more bulky in the hip-length bearskin coat. The chill had drained color from his face till the flesh formed a chalky contrast to the bluish sheen of his brutal jaw. Behind the man, Rockwall saw Pedro. Graves moved into the tack room, white teeth flashing in his grin.

"You did get them, didn't you, kid?" he said. "This was almost too easy."

He was looking at Rockwall, and in the man's eyes Rockwall read the end of this. Graves would take no halfway chances now, so close to the finish. He turned to say to Pedro: "Get the roan out now, and make it snappy."

Rockwall was standing almost against the stove, and its heat was making him uncomfortable. But it put an idea in his mind. It was just about the only chance for a break they had left.

"So you're going to give Tie money," he said.

Graves turned back to him, vague surprise flitting through his eyes. "That's right . . . and it's a fair split," he answered. "Tie's through with Aldis, after seeing her with you."

"You're a fool, kid, to think he'll hand over that much money," Rockwall told Tie. "He'll squeeze you out as soon as he sees the chance."

"Hobble your jaw, Rockwall," Graves said.

But the pressure Tie was struggling under was patent in his shining eyes and compressed lips— the realization of how much he had lost in this game, his rage at Rockwall, his youthful desire for revenge, his anger with himself for having been such a fool. Rockwall wondered just how much it would take to make him snap.

"What good's the money going to do, even if you get it?" he asked Tie. "You still want Aldis, and you know it."

The boy's lips twitched. "Shut up, Del!"

"*Señor* Kenny!" Pedro called fearfully, from down the aisle. "I can't get no hobbles on thees blue devil. He'll kick my head in."

"Go help him, Tie," Graves ordered.

"Sure," Rockwall told Tie. "Go help them get the horse, help Graves get Aldis . . ."

"Damn you, Rockwall!" The boy's voice held that shrill overtone again. "Shut up!"

"You know you can't go through with this, kid," Rockwall said hurriedly. "Can you face Aldis when Graves brings in the roan, can you just stand there and watch Jennings hand Aldis over to Graves?"

"God damn you!" Tie shouted.

"Tie!"

Graves's angry shout was too late. The boy had already jumped at Rockwall, whipping the Hopkins up. Rockwall threw an arm in front of himself to block the blow. The barrel struck his elbow, numbing his arm. He let the blow drive him back against the stove. He could not help crying out with the pain of red-hot iron hissing against his Levi's. But his weight knocked the stove over. He struck it again as he fell, and tried to throw himself to the side to keep from being burned. Sprawled across the floor, he heard the crash as the stove hit the puncheons, and then the stovepipe came down in sections.

A hot section hit him across the legs, and he cried out in pain. But he was already coming to his hands and knees. He had a dim impression of Kammas, struggling with Tie off to the right, and of Graves lunging backward and pawing beneath his bearskin coat for a gun. Rockwall lunged at the man from hands and knees, striking him waist-high, and carrying him backward out through the door. Graves was knocked over and they rolled together into the barn.

With his face buried in that stinking bearskin, Rockwall heard the pounding of feet coming this way from the roan's stall. Then a blow caught him on the head from behind. It drove him flat across Graves. Through vast miles of pain, he heard Tie calling.

"Graves, it's on fire! The whole room's on fire!"

"Get the horse, then! Hurry up, you knot-heads, get that roan out of here!"

Rockwall could no longer feel Graves beneath him, and knew the man must have squirmed out. He tried to get to his hands and knees. He could hear nothing now but a great roaring. Then that engulfed him and the lights went out.

Chapter Seventeen

When Rockwall regained consciousness, his first sensations were of pain. His hip, his ribs, all along his right side seemed to be on fire. There was a great throbbing at the base of his neck. He opened his eyes. All around him it was white. He was borne on some cottony substance, and, whenever he moved, he seemed to sink into it.

Finally he realized he was lying in the snow. He tried to sit up. Hands helped him. Kammas. Rockwall raised his head and finally found the old man, partly behind him, supporting him. Then he realized they were sitting in the snow on the slope above the house and barn. The barn was almost burned down now. Only part of one wall remained, with the flames licking half-heartedly up its snow-dampened siding. The rest was a black stain of ashes and smoldering embers against the virginal mantle of snow.

"That was a right smart idee, making Tie hit you so you could knock over the stove," Kammas said.

Rockwall stared dully at the barn. "I figured they'd have their hands full getting that horse out if there was a fire, and maybe we'd have a chance to do something. How did we get out of it?"

"I saw that Mex hit you from behind with his gun," Kammas said. "Just after that Tie knocked me back against the wall and I banged my head. It didn't knock me out, but I played 'possum. By that time the fire was going too good for them to worry about us. I pulled you through the back door while they was all fighting with the horse. The tack room and the whole rear section was burning roof high by the time they got the roan out. They must have thought we got burned to death."

"The other animals?"

"Tie's too good a horseman to stand by and see critters burn. He turned 'em out before the front end of the barn caved in. The chestnut and 'Bakker got away and headed for that timber south of the house."

Rockwall looked up at him. "We've got to find them."

Kammas frowned. "You don't mean to go after that bunch. We ain't got a gun between us, Rockwall."

"We can't wait. It isn't only the horse. Tie's use to Graves is done now."

"Are you still thinking of that kid . . . after all he's done to you?"

"Graves was going to kill us, Kammas," Rockwall said, getting unsteadily to his feet. "He would have if the fire hadn't got in his way. He's capable of doing the same thing to Tie."

Kammas spat disgustedly. "He ain't worth saving."

Rockwall stared at him. "Do you really believe that?"

Kammas tried to meet his eyes, then dropped his gaze miserably. "Hell, Rockwall, how can you be so soft?"

"If you won't do it for Tie, think about the roan. Can you sit up here and let Graves hand Blue Boy over to Jennings?"

Kammas's head jerked up. "All right. Let's get the horses."

It took them an hour to locate the animals, following their trail through timber and drifts, up over the ridge behind the house and down into the next deep valley. 'Bakker was saddled, but the chestnut was bare. They rode back to the house for coats and a blanket to strap on the chestnut. It was the best they could do, since all the rigging had been burned in the barn. Then they took out on the trail of Graves. By the tracks, it was evident that the men had been forced to keep the roan in hobbles, and even then it was fighting them every step of the way. This would cut down their time greatly. Rockwall had the desperate hope that he would come up with them in time.

"And what do we do when we catch them?" Kammas complained. "Bare hands ain't no good."

"Maybe we can cut around ahead of them and get a couple of guns off the cook at the Forked Tongue," Rockwall muttered. "Most of the crew should be out in the line shacks now, and that cook never was in much shape for a fight."

Rockwall cut directly through the drifts, slanting as nearly as he could in a direct line in an effort to make up for lost time. They cut the trails left by Graves and his party several times. There were three horses and the roan. Then only two horses and the roan.

They dropped down into the creek bottom in Black Rock Cañon, where the drifts were not quite so deep. They passed the old line shack as they angled up the slope to the rim, and cut the trail left by Graves and his party once more. Kammas took one look and halted his mare.

"Met a rider here," he said quietly. "Now there's three again."

"I see it," said Rockwall. "We'll have to go back."

Kammas nodded silent assent and they turned south again. There was a tightness in Rockwall's throat, and he was cursing himself with weary bitterness. For a while he had hoped Graves was going to wait until he reached the Forked Tongue, and because of this he had dared to take the short cuts. Now he knew the gamble had failed.

"Just ahead," Kammas said from behind him. Then the old man's voice rose on a furious note. "That damned Graves didn't finish him! There's a trail leading off the road."

Rockwall sprang down hurriedly and plunged into the snow. The track Tie had left zigzagged away from the road for 100 feet. Then Rockwall came to the boy. Tie was down on his face. There were two bullet holes in his back. Gently Rockwall turned him over. Under the Mackinaw, the whole front of him was fresh with blood. His eyes fluttered, opened.

"You were right," he said faintly. "Graves wanted everything for himself."

"Don't try to talk."

"That's all I got left, Del. Just a few words. Can I switch ends once more?"

"How do you mean, kid?"

"I'm sorry, Del. Really sorry now."

"I believe you. It's just hell you had to learn the hard way."

"That's it." Tie tried to laugh. Blood bubbled into his mouth and he choked on it. His coughing seemed to drain the life from him. He sagged back against the snow. "That's it. You were waiting for me to learn my lesson, weren't you? Waiting for me to grow up."

"I knew you weren't bad at the bottom. They just gave you too big a horse to handle the first time."

"Tell Aldis I'm sorry, too." The words left Tie in a whisper. Then he surged up against Rockwall, eyes wild. "I'm going to ride that roan in the morning, Del. I can feel it in my bones, I'm going to top that blue devil."

"Tie . . ."

The crescendo of their voices broke off like a snapped stick, with the echoes slapping down the avenues of timber to die a muffled death against the snowbanks beyond. Rockwall lowered the boy back down, staring a moment at the face, young and at peace now, with its closed eyes. Kammas stood back of Rockwall, breathing huskily. At last Rockwall rose.

"Loose rocks down by the creek," he said in a hollow voice. "That's the best place. He'll be safe from the wolves. We can't dig a grave, but if we pile them high enough, it'll be just as good."

Chapter Eighteen

They rode afterward like men pursued, forcing their flagging horses to the utmost. Rockwall had found his own gun in Tie's holster, and Kammas had found Graves's Derringer in the Mackinaw pocket, so they were both armed again. They followed the old logging road down out of the ridges to where it joined the Hellgate road, and pushed their animals west along this till they reached the cut-off to the Forked Tongue.

When they came into sight of that house up on the knob, there was light by the corrals, the bobbing glow of bull's-eye lanterns, blocked out again and again by the black silhouettes of moving men.

Rockwall and Kammas dropped off the flats into the creek bottom, the horses' hoofs slipping and clattering across slick rocks and icy shelves. Finally the chestnut went down on the rocks, and Rockwall had to take a dive at a snowbank.

Kammas swung off and tied the mare to some chokecherry. Rockwall secured the chestnut. Then they scrambled up the steep bank, through skeleton poplars and clumps of pussy willows that rattled like old bones against their legs. Rockwall kept his right hand inside the worn coat he had got from the house, hoping that would be enough warmth to keep it supple.

They reached the fringe of trees and saw the back ends of the barns 100 yards ahead of them. The pair of hip-roofed buildings blocked them off from the corrals. Rockwall glanced at Kammas. The old man nodded grimly. Rockwall broke from cover, heading in a slogging run for the rear of the first barn.

His head seemed empty now. He was left with the sense of awesome inevitability, as if following out some plan that had been ordained for him long ago. They were within fifty feet of the buildings when a man appeared on the knoll, heading down toward the corrals. He stopped and his shout was raised sharply against the chill night air.

"Jennings, somebody's coming up behind the barns!"

Rockwall half turned toward the man with a curse. Then he wheeled back to Kammas. "You go around the south end here. I'll go through the middle if that door's open. Hit them from both sides."

He reached the door and shoved. It made a raucous *squeak,* swinging open before his weight. The front door was partly open, the space turned to a flickering rectangle by the light of lanterns outside. Into this half-lit opening came the figure of a running man. He must have heard Rockwall's pounding feet, for he brought up with a startled yell, and Rockwall saw the flicker of light run along a gun barrel.

The sound of the shot boomed through the barn. Rockwall heard the bullet smash into wood on his left. A horse screamed in wild fright and began crashing against its stall. He had his own gun up by then, and its sound blotted out the noises of the horse for one smashing instant. The man's silhouette lifted upward, and then dropped off into the black shadows of the ground.

Rockwall ran down to the front door. The man sprawled on the ground there was Pedro, the bartender from the Sapphire. The bullet had caught him squarely, and he was dead.

From the door Rockwall could see a pair of corrals about 100 feet to the right of the barn. The nearest was a large holding pen, and beyond that was a smaller breaking corral. They were separated by a narrow alleyway. This was blocked up at its far end by a chute that joined a pen with the corral. And in that upper corral they had put Blue Boy.

The rest of the men had been gathered on the

far side of the enclosures, near that chute. But now Rockwall could see their fluttery movements, cutting down the far fence of the nearest pen. He knew he would be trapped in the barn once they reached the corner and had a clear shot at him, so he made his jump while the pole fences still stood between him and the running men.

"There he is!" shouted Jennings. "Just coming out of the barn! Get him, Graves, get him!"

The smashing volley of shots they threw at him was wild, and Rockwall reached the fence unhurt, jumping behind a heavy upright. The alleyway separating the two enclosures was on his left now. There was a flash of movement at its far end, where the chute closed it up, joining the two enclosures. Through the maze of poles Rockwall saw lantern light flicker tawnily across Graves's bearskin coat. He realized that Graves was crawling through the bars of the chute to come down to this end of the alley. Before Rockwall could raise his gun, there was a furtive tattoo of feet on his right.

He wheeled toward the lower end of the big pen. Baxter already stood there with his gun lined up. In that last moment, Rockwall felt his own responses twitching his gun around, and knew he was a million years too late.

Then Kammas came around the corner of the barn and shot Baxter. The albino foreman's shot went wild as he was smashed back against the fence. He slid down till he sat on the ground, clutching a bloody shoulder.

"Douse the lanterns, you knot-heads!" Graves shouted. "He's over by the holding pen!"

There was a harsh *tinkle* of breaking glass and one of the lights went out. Blue Boy was trotting around inside the upper corral, snorting and squealing.

"Kenny, watch out!" cried Aldis from somewhere.

"Shut up, you little tramp," snarled Jennings, and then there was a sharp cry. Rockwall felt anger pull his lips against his teeth. He looked over a shoulder to see that Kammas was coming to join him, carrying Baxter's gun.

"Graves is somewhere over by that chute between the two pens," Rockwall whispered. "You take it around by Baxter's corner. I'll go up this way."

A lantern still glowed from somewhere beyond the pens. Its light only served to deepen the nearer shadows, lying black and viscid beneath the fences. Blue Boy seemed to be making the only sound now, running the bars.

"Baxter!" shouted Jennings suddenly. "That you?"

"Shut up, you fool!" answered Graves.

That was right ahead. Rockwall moved faster. He was a foot from the corner when he caught the faintest of movements just beyond the corner. He jumped around it and caught Potter, coming up off his knees, gun in hand. Rockwall let his impetus carry him into the man, bringing up one knee. He knocked the gun skyward as it went off. Potter tried to come on up off his knees against Rockwall, grappling him. Rockwall whipped his gun across the man's face.

Potter fell back. There was a fluttery movement from the other side of the chute at the far end of the alley. A shot smashed at Rockwall, chipping wood off into his face. He flattened himself against the fence so hard the corral shuddered. The horizontal poles were lashed to the inside of the fence posts. That left a body thickness of upright behind which he could stand. In the dark shadows, he was invisible to the man beyond the chute as long as he did not move. But Potter was moaning heavily now and rolling over.

"Graves!" shouted Jennings. "Where are you?"

Jennings's voice startled Rockwall, coming from the other direction. Graves's answer was hoarse and tense.

"I think he's in that alley between the two pens! The chute blocks off this end! You come down the west side of Blue Boy's corral and we'll have him between us!"

Rockwall cast a last look at the faint pattern of chute bars, striving to see Graves behind them. It was too dark. He heard the soft sound of feet lining down the west side of the roan's corral. In another minute Jennings would be at that corner, and he would be pinched off between them.

The frantic tattoo of the roan's trotting hoofs approached him. The horse seemed to be coming down on the inside of the west fence. Jennings's presence right behind was driving the beast, then. And when he hit the corner, he would turn down the corral parallel to the alley. The thought gave Rockwall a last dim hope.

At that moment Potter sat up, shaking his head sickly. He looked around, and even in the darkness Rockwall could see his mouth gape open as the man realized his position. He started to rise, bawling fearfully.

"Graves, don't shoot! You'll hit me!"

Realizing that would give his position away as much as anything else, Rockwall made the last move left to him. He lunged across the alley for the fence of the roan's pen. The roan hit the corner about the same time and wheeled to run down this fence. A shot smashed from the chute, digging up earth a foot behind Rockwall's running form.

"Graves!" screamed Potter. "You'll hit me!"

Rockwall smashed against the poles as he stooped to duck through. The horse was going by fast on the inside. He wheeled wildly, lashing a hind hoof at Rockwall. Rockwall dodged the hoof, lunging for the roan. He caught his halter before it could get away from him. He tried to rear up, but Rockwall held him down. This started the animal into a frenzied run, dragging him along, with the horse between himself and the alley fence.

"Graves!" yelled Jennings. "Where is he?"

"Still in the alley somewhere!" Graves shouted. "I've lost sight of him!"

Hanging onto the halter, Rockwall tried to keep up with the horse. He ran madly for a few stumbling paces, with the beast half dragging him down the inside of the alley fence straight toward the chute at its other end. The animal's wild movements covered his own in those last moments. He was almost at the chute when he could no longer keep his feet. He let go the halter and was falling as the horse ran out from between him and the fence. He had an instantaneous glimpse of Graves, right on the other side of the fence.

The man was wheeling, mouth open in shocked surprise as he saw how he had been fooled. Rockwall fired as he fell, just once. He saw Graves's heavy body jerk violently.

Then Rockwall hit the ground, hard, and flopped helplessly over and over till he came to a stop against the fence. Stunned, he saw Graves sliding down against the bars of the chute, his face contorted.

"Graves!" bellowed Jennings. "What are you shooting at? He isn't in this alley!"

"No, Jennings," Kammas said. "But I am. Right behind you. Drop your gun."

The only sound after that was the excited beat of the roan's hoofs, up at the other end of the corral. Graves lay huddled against the chute now, eyes open and glazed in death. Rockwall got up and walked down toward the other side of the corral, stooping through the poles into the alley. Jennings stood there, with Potter still sitting against the fence, bent over sickly.

At this moment Aldis came running around the corner, calling Graves's name. She stopped abruptly, shaking heavily, when she saw Rockwall. "Kenny said you'd been burned in the barn," she said curtly.

Rockwall looked at her. "Graves killed Tie. We buried him along the creek in Black Rock Cañon. Now Graves is dead."

She looked at him with tear-shining eyes, suddenly unable to put into words what she felt.

Rockwall stayed there while he called to the other hands. There was no fight left in them, with Graves dead and Jennings disarmed. They came in one by one, allowing Kammas to disarm them. Then Rockwall looked at Kammas, and the old man nodded, turning up toward the corral gate. Jennings was breathing heavily with a terrible, frustrated anger.

"What's Kammas doing?" he asked.

"Letting Blue Boy loose," Rockwall said.

Rage swelled Jennings's neck. "Rockwall, you can't do this to me, you . . ." The big man broke off suddenly, face twisted, and then wheeled and started to run out of the alley after Kammas. Rockwall's gun snapped up beside Aldis's body, roaring. The bullet kicked up dirt to one side of Jenning's right boot. It halted him so sharply he almost fell.

"If you take another step, I'll shoot your legs out from under you," Rockwall said.

Jennings had caught the fence to keep from falling. He stared back at Rockwall, shuddering now with the terrible emotion that gripped him. Then there was the *creak* of a gate, and Kammas called to his Blue Boy. The pound of hoofs was like the tattoo of a triumphant drum. The horse passed through the gate like a shadow in the darkness. There was a last wild bugling call. Then he was gone.

Jennings's whole great body seemed to shrink. A million lines etched themselves deeply into a face turned the color of parchment.

Aldis bowed her head against her chest. Rockwall looked over her head to Jennings. "Kammas and I are heading out," he said. "And, by God, you'd better not come after us."

Rockwall saw this final defeat was robbing the man of life. Jennings drew a wheezing breath, started to say something, then his shoulders sagged. He turned and went out of the alley and across the compound toward the house. He looked indescribably old and beaten. Kammas came back, casting only a glance at Jennings. Aldis turned and ran after Jennings's retreating form.

"Want to go to Texas?" Rockwall asked Kammas.

"You'll make out," Kammas said. "Ain't a man north of the Gulf wouldn't jump at the chance to have you work his horses. You'll even have that ranch of yours someday. I wish I could go with you. But I wouldn't fit. Four walls make me jumpy. I'll be out in the Strip if you ever come back this way, Rockwall." He sobered, squinting. "Think maybe, come spring, I'll get another look at the Blue Boy?"

"Sure," Rockwall said gently. "A lot of looks."

Kammas tried to grin and failed.

"Maybe, if you won't go, I'll stay here. There's a lot of wild ones still to catch. What say we head out to your camp?"

"I'll get your horse," Kammas said. Now he was grinning. He turned to hobble off toward the creek and the horses.

Rockwall asked one of the men for the loan of a saddle. The other hands went to take care of Baxter.

As Rockwall and Kammas rode away from the Forked Tongue, Rockwall took a last look back. The front door of the ranch house was open and he saw her in that yellow rectangle of the door before the timber swallowed them. He tried to read defeat in the lines of her silhouette, standing there, watching the end of everything she had tried to gain by playing so many ends against the middle. But, somehow, he could not find defeat. She seemed as unbridled, as defiant as ever. She was like Blue Boy. One man could never hold her. Probably no man ever would.

About the Author

Les Savage, Jr. was born in Alhambra, California and grew up in Los Angeles. His first published story was "Bullets and Bullwhips" accepted by the prestigious magazine, Street & Smith's *Western Story*. Almost ninety more magazine stories followed, all set on the American frontier, many of them published in Fiction House magazines such as *Frontier Stories* and *Lariat Story Magazine* where Savage became a superstar with his name on many covers. His first novel, *Treasure of the Brasada*, appeared from Simon & Schuster in 1947. Due to his preference for historical accuracy, Savage often ran into problems with book editors in the 1950s who were concerned about marriages between his protagonists and women of different races—a commonplace on the real frontier but not in much Western fiction in that decade. Savage died young, at thirty-five, from complications arising out of hereditary diabetes and elevated cholesterol. However, as a result of the censorship imposed on many of his works, only now are they being fully restored by returning to the author's original manuscripts. Among Savage's finest Western stories are *Fire Dance at Spider Rock*, *Medicine Wheel*, *Coffin Gap*, *Phantoms in the Night*, *The Bloody Quarter*, *In The Land of Little Sticks*, *The Cavan Breed*, and *Danger Rides the River*. Much as Stephen Crane before him, while he wrote, the shadow of his imminent death grew longer and longer across his young life, and he knew that, if he was going to do it at all, he would have to do it quickly. He did it well, and, now that his novels and stories are being restored to what he had intended them to be, his achievement irradiated by his powerful and profoundly sensitive imagination will be with us always, as he had wanted it to be, as he had so rushed against time and mortality that it might be.

Center Point Publishing
600 Brooks Road • PO Box 1
Thorndike ME 04986-0001 USA

(207) 568-3717

US & Canada:
1 800 929-9108
www.centerpointlargeprint.com